SON OF MY LOVE

...the kingdom of the Son of His love

Colossians 1:13, The Amplified Bible

author SUE SHARP

Leeway Literary Works
Published by Leeway Artisans, Inc.

Book & Cover Design by Mykle Lee

ISBN: 978-0-9846698-3-7

First Edition
Printed in the United States of America.

FOREWORD

If an anthology is a collection of writings that can either be read as a continuing narrative or as stories that can stand alone, then <u>Son of My Love</u> is indeed an anthology. Sue Sharp, Kentucky author and longtime friend, has opened a window into the time of Jesus and His journey. The ordinary-looking craftsman of the Nazareth carpenter shop is brought to readers of the twenty-first century in a unique and caring narrative that dispels mysticism and portrays Him as the very human/very divine Son of God. The story takes place on the other side, in Heaven, as well as on Earth, as the battle between the evil forces and the Creator gears up.

Sue has written from a desire to explore the relationship between Father and Son. She believes if we understand how much they cared for each other, it could help us understand a little better how high a price each of them paid for our salvation.

To know this author is to know a real Kentucky treasure. Appalled by the current glorification of Satan, she has taken on the daunting task of writing between the lines. Of giving the reader her take of how the history of man plays out in the full power of his Creator.

She has listened well to the nuances in the gospels, and has set down a rendering of the behind-the-scenes look we've all wondered about.

Almost all writers call upon divine inspiration at one time or another. Her writing just happens to be about the Divine who hands down the inspiration. This book is important because it takes a stand. It is written earnestly and from the heart and soul of a person who walks with the Lord on a daily basis. To be in the company of Sue Sharp is to enjoy an uplifting moment. In a hectic and torn world, there is nothing more comforting than being with a person who says what she believes, and sometimes uses song in a discussion to illustrate her point if the conversation has led in that direction.

She is confident she has been handed a story to tell, and has done so.

My hope for this book is that it touches lives, one at a time, and helps them to turn to God for strength and peace.

Jerrie Oughton, author
Washington, North Carolina

Dedicated to my mother,
Esta Bell Sharp,
And to
My elementary school teacher,
Grace Ellenburg Margrave
Both those ladies taught me
By their lives how very much
God cares for the least of us,
And for all of us.

A resident of Kentucky since the late Fifties, Sue Sharp was born and raised in east Tennessee. Her father was a coal miner and her mother a homemaker. She is the youngest of five siblings. Since 1960 she has been a member of Trinity Baptist Church in Lexington, where she taught Sunday School for 34 years. She is a choir member and, with a friend from Immanuel Baptist, sings in church-sponsored services in local nursing homes. Sue has a series of Christian mystery novels planned. One is completed, and two others are in progress.

PROLOGUE

God stood quietly in the silent Throne Room of Heaven. In a few moments His beloved only Son would leave Home for thirty-three years of earthly struggle. At the end of that struggle waited a Roman cross, with all the physical agony, humiliation, and abandonment bound up in that hideous death.

Tears filled the Father's eyes as He looked at the young man waiting for Michael to appear at the door with the announcement that it was time for Him to go. Pain and abandonment had never touched the Prince of Heaven. He had always been safe here in Immanuel's Land, protected by the full force of His Father's power. A vengeful, jealous Satan wanted nothing so much as to have God's adored Son in his eager clutches. He was lurking, claws unsheathed, in Bethlehem. Eventually he would catch up with the Prince in the wilderness after

Jesus' baptism. Finally he would dig his claws, in the shape of Roman nails, into Jesus' body.

God spoke, not in the thundering voice that shook Earth's frame, but in a voice laden with tenderness. "You know, Son, that if there were any other way, you would not be leaving here. But my own nature prohibits me from taking man's sin on myself."

"Yes, I know how much you want to spare me. In a way, it will be harder for you, watching what they will do to me. Wanting to rescue me and knowing you can't-- not and accomplish what we both want to do."

"I want you to understand that you may still decline to go. Understand, too, that you may leave Earth and come back Home whenever you choose, with no reprimand or punishment. I would love you no less. That is not possible."

Michael entered the Throne Room. Misery was etched in every line of the archangel's face. Michael did not know—and would not know until Crucifixion Day—what was planned for his Prince and Friend. But he knew Satan's hatred for the Son of God.

Michael bowed. "I'm sorry, Your Majesty. It's almost time for the Prince to leave. Gabriel is ready in the Council Chamber."

"Just a few more moments with my Son, Michael. We will be out soon."

Michael bowed again and left. God turned back to Jesus. "Be sure that you think the human race is really worth what you are going to go through."

Jesus' gaze fastened on His Father's face. "They're worth it; and even if I didn't think so, you do. That is what matters most to me."

"Always be on your guard, my Son. Satan will strike when you are hungry and tired, or lonely, or when people disappoint you. Sometimes all those things will happen to you at once. I have given you the best parents I can find, but even your mother will misunderstand you at times."

"With your help, I can endure whatever Satan brings against me."

"You're aware that the time will come when even I will be forced to abandon you. For the first time in your life, I will not be with you. When I walk away, you must keep totally focused on why you came to Earth, and hold on to everything you know about me. That is the only way your soul will survive." God wrapped His arms around His Son. "For thousands of years I have watched other fathers send their sons off to war to protect things that are precious and sacred. And now it is my turn, and my Son who must go."

They walked, the Father's arm around the Son's shoulders, toward the Throne Room door. God stopped just inside the door and turned to speak to His Son face to face. "You are my only Soldier in this battle, and the only Defender mankind has. Whatever fears you may face, whatever other doubts Satan tries to plant in your soul, never doubt how much I love you."

CHAPTER ONE

Sonlight and Starlight

A SAD-FACED ARIEL STOPPED another angel on Coronation Plaza. "Have you heard, Tobias?" he asked his friend. "The Prince is leaving. He won't be coming Home for years, if ever."

His unimpressed friend flicked a stray sprinkle of gold dust from a glistening feather of one of his wings. "That rumor has been floating around ever since Adam and Eve were driven from the Garden."

"I don't know, Tobias. Something is going on. The archangels have been coming and going from the Council Chamber all day. And I heard Gabriel say a few days ago that things were almost ready, that the Romans have finally completed their network of roads, so travel will be faster and easier. And the Pax Romana is in full force."

"Force is right," sniffed Tobias. "Brute force. Those Romans are the cruelest bunch to walk the earth since the Babylonians dragged the Father's people away with hooks in their mouths hundreds of years ago."

"That's why the Father wants the Prince to go down there," Ariel insisted, "to try to put a stop to the cruelty."

"That will never happen." Tobias, sure now that he had his friend where he wanted him in the discussion, smiled a slightly superior smile. "You know how the Father dotes on that Boy. He knows Lucifer is down there waiting, hoping to lure the Prince away from His Father's protection. Lucifer will tear the Boy to pieces if he ever gets his devious hands on Him. You heard Lucifer screaming he would do exactly that as they were throwing him out of here for starting a revolt."

Tobias waved a friendly greeting to Daniel as the prophet crossed the Plaza. The angel had a special warm spot in his heart for Daniel. The prophet always seemed appreciative of Tobias' gallant effort to come to his aid years ago, when Tobias had battled the wicked angel of Persia to carry the Father's word of reassurance to Daniel. It had been a little embarrassing, Tobias recalled, that he and the Persian angel had been so evenly matched that he had had to call in Archangel Michael to help him. Michael and Daniel had both been nice enough not to mention it to him, though.

Ariel's voice drew him back to the present. "I declare, Tobias, it has been like a funeral here since that Council meeting has been going on." He made a wry face. "I hate that word--funeral. I'm glad we don't need the word here. Don't know why I thought of it."

Tobias glanced down at a garden on the slope of a Judean hillside. Workmen were carving a tomb in the rock for Joseph of Arimathea, although Joseph would not need it for years yet. Tobias sighed. "I know, Ariel. I don't like the word, either."

Elnathan walked up to join them. "From the look on your face, Ariel, I see you've heard about the proposal."

Ariel's troubled face went uncharacteristically blank. "Proposal?"

"Yes. From Lucifer. Again. How many centuries has he been trying? He even had the gall to sign it 'Satan.' Just to taunt the Father, apparently."

"He always was arrogant," Tobias broke in. "His exaggerated opinion of himself is what got him into trouble in the first place. He's only holding mankind hostage to get back at the Father. I don't know what he expects to gain by it."

"Revenge," answered Elnathan. "As usual, Lucifer says he wants to trade the human race for Prince Yeshua."

"I know the Father cares deeply about man." Tobias shook his shining head. "But He will never hand His Son over to Lucifer's--maybe I should say Satan's-- savagery."

Elnathan took his leave of them. The carved ivory doors of the Council Chamber swung open. Somber and subdued, Gabriel cut across to the edge of Coronation Plaza. His eyes searched the little backwater corner of the Roman Empire called Galilee until he located the dusty village of Nazareth. Then he spread his powerful wings and dove earthward.

The Father and the Prince, in a conversation so deep that They were oblivious to everything around Them, walked to the parapet that topped the high wall surrounding the City. They stood almost in arm's length of the angels, yet Ariel and Tobias could not hear the discussion. Not wanting to intrude on an obviously serious, private matter between Father and Son, the angels refrained from moving closer.

Prince Yeshua suddenly lifted the glimmering diadem from His head and handed it to His Father. The meaning of that act hit Tobias like a blow to the head. Screaming "No!" he lunged at the young Prince, clutching desperately at the sleeve of His white linen robe.

The Father put a restraining hand on Tobias' arm. "Let Him go, Tobias."

"Lord, please stop Him! You know Satan is down there, and he'll find Him!"

"I know, Tobias, and so does He. But this is what He wants. Let Him go."

The Father gently untangled Tobias' grasping fingers from the Prince's sleeve and drew His Son close to Him. Yeshua embraced His Father. Then, in a nuclear-bright supernova of light, He was gone.

The proud Father, tears staining His face, was left holding the diadem. Yeshua's magnificent robe was draped over His arm.

The courtyard was deathly quiet, except for Tobias' soul-deep sobs. Ariel, too grief-stunned to even weep, stood like a piece of statuary.

Son of My Love

The Father and the two angels turned to look over the parapet. Tobias stared down at Nazareth. "Are those two going to be His parents, Lord?"

"Yes. Their names are Joseph and Mary."

"They're too young to protect Him, Your Majesty."

"That is why I want the two of you to look after Him. Give Him complete protection, until the day I tell you to withdraw that protection. From then on, He will have to walk the rest of the way by Himself. Even I won't be able to help Him."

"How long will He survive, Lord?" Ariel finally dared to ask.

"Thirty-three of their years." He added softly, to Himself, "And every day to the Lord is as a thousand years." Tears filled His eyes again. "All those days. All those long days."

Ariel, trying to offer some shred of comfort, said to the Father, "It's a terrible ransom to pay, but if anyone can liberate mankind, it's Prince Yeshua."

"If anyone liberates mankind," the Father answered, "it will have to be Prince Yeshua. There is no one else." He smoothed the gold embroidery on the linen robe lovingly. "From now on, I want Him to be called 'Jesus.'"

Tobias reached for the robe and diadem. "Let me put those away, Your Majesty, so you won't have to look at them."

"Thank you, but I will put them away. I want to close off His palace."

He turned to face the East and lifted His hand. Out on the edge of the universe, an enormous explosion of light invaded the darkness and congealed into a star larger than any the two angels had ever seen. The star began moving at a slow, majestic pace toward the constellation of Leo.

"The Light shines in the darkness," the Father said. "I made certain that He understood He did not have to go through with this." He turned the diadem around in His hands, watching tiny flashes of crystal fire play among the priceless gems. "Someday, people will call His birthday Christmas. Perhaps someday they will stop, amid all their rushing around and spending. Maybe they will even stop long enough to think about how much We spent on Our Gift for them."

CHAPTER TWO

Nazareth

Two young boys argued loudly in a village street. Their voices ruptured the early-morning quiet and drifted through the window of a workshop, where one boy's oldest brother was working. The argument escalated into an exchange of insults. One of the boys shoved the other, and a scuffle began, with the boys rolling around in the dusty village street. Suddenly one of the boys seemed to levitate off the ground. He found himself dangling a good two feet above the street, courtesy of his oldest brother's firm grip around his waist.

The older brother set the younger on his feet. The ten-year-old, doing a quick mental calculation of how many times he had been the object of big-brotherly discipline the past week, searched the man's tanned face for an indication of just how much trouble he was in. Talking back was out of the question. Years of carving stone and cutting and shaping lumber had given the young man a strength that His slim build belied.

The man helped the neighbor boy up out of the dirt. "Are you hurt?" He asked the boy He had helped to his feet. The question was more an expression of courtesy than concern, because the youngster was obviously not injured.

"I'm all right," he answered as he dusted himself off, "but my mother won't like it because I'm so dirty."

The man's brother adopted what he hoped sounded like a reasonable tone. "He started it. It's his fault he got dirty."

"I saw you through the window, Simon. I know you shoved Isaac."

"But he said--"

"I heard what he said. If he behaves like that again, I will take the matter up with his father. As for you, this is the second time in three days that I have had to stop working to handle a fight involving you. You know I don't want you fighting, unless you have to defend yourself. If this happens again, I'm going to apply some serious discipline. I'll leave it to your imagination as to what that will be. Now go check on your little sister."

"Yes, Sir," Simon mumbled, disappointed. He had hoped to see Isaac get what he considered a fair share of the lecture.

The man turned His attention to the other young gladiator. "Isaac, I think your mother would like you home now."

Knowing that his parents would exact punishment if he spoke disrespectfully to the popular young Carpenter, Isaac added his own mumbled "Yes, Sir" to Simon's and trudged away down the dusty street, his sandals stirring up little puff clouds of dry brown dirt.

A slender woman struggled to carry a heavy bucket of water over the threshold. The man reached out to take the bucket from her. "Good morning, mother. I'll take that for you."

"Thank you. It gets heavier with every step." She caught her breath. "I went to the well as early as I could, before the day got hotter."

"You should have made James bring the water before he left."

"Before you can get James to do anything, you have to find him."

The man set the bucket on the table in the kitchen and returned to work. He carved and smoothed the rough boards, enjoying watching them take shape in His hands. He lost Himself in the work, politely declining His mother's request that He stop to eat. She brought Him a cup of water and left Him to His task.

The shadows moving across the wall marked off another hour spent at the bench. His head snapped up as a sense of imminent danger flashed across His consciousness. He dropped the saw and left the shop, running toward the hill at the end of the street. His seven-year-old sister was crawling around the hill, trying to capture a bright yellow bird hopping around the rim of the cliff.

Not wanting to startle her into losing her balance, He restrained the impulse to call out to her. She was so intent on catching the bird that she did not hear His running footsteps.

He snatched her up in His arms and spun her away from the edge. "Joanna, how many times have we told you to stay away from this hill?" He demanded angrily. "You could have slipped and fallen over!"

"I just wanted to catch the pretty bird and show it to mother. I wouldn't have hurt it. Please don't be mad at me," she pleaded tearfully, trying to divert His attention from her disobedience.

"That tactic won't work, young lady. We're going to talk about your disobeying and putting yourself in danger." He knelt to talk to her on her level. "Yes, I'm angry with you. Everyone in the family has told you to stay away from here, that the hill is dangerous."

"Are you going to spank me? You never have before."

"Not this time, but if you come back, you will leave me no choice. I can't allow you to endanger yourself and anyone who might try to help you. If you do this again, both of us are going to be very unhappy."

"I'll stay away from the hill," she answered solemnly.

"Good. Don't forget promising me that."

"What are you going to do about this time?"

"I'm taking you home. You're going to stay in your own yard the rest of the day."

"Yessir," she readily agreed.

Jesus looked around at the hill. The bird was nowhere to be found. There were no trees or bushes nearby to hide it, and its bright yellow color would make it easy to see out in the open. Anger, this time not at Joanna's disobedience, turned His dark eyes even darker. He put His arm protectively around His sister's shoulders. *Not this time, Satan,* He thought. *This is at least one child you won't get your claws on.*

He led Joanna home and went back to work. Late in the afternoon He set aside His regular work and put the finishing touches on a handsomely carved wooden bowl. He set the bowl on a shelf just as His mother appeared in the doorway to issue an order.

"Enough for now, young man. Come inside and rest."

He sat down at the table and helped Himself to cheese and bread. His mother took a chair across from Him and resumed her sewing.

"I'm glad to have a few minutes to talk to you, Son. You have spent so many hours working this past week that we haven't had time to talk. You really should stop and rest more."

He ran his hand through His dark brown hair and laughed. "The children usually provide me with at least one diversion a day, mother."

"You still have been working too many hours. You look exhausted. James should help you more. And the three other boys are all old enough to take on more chores."

"I let James go to Sepphoris with Benjamin this morning. But starting tomorrow, he is going to start working in the shop every day instead of a few days a week, even if he doesn't work a full day."

"I still miss meeting you and Joseph in Sepphoris, even though it's been a long time. When the two of you were cutting stone for the buildings on the marketplace square, Elizabeth and I would walk over sometimes and go through the bazaars, then walk home with you. She was always fascinated by the people from the caravans, with all their different languages and dress."

Jesus poured goat's milk from a pitcher and offered it to her. She shook her head, and He kept the cup. "The way she went from one booth to another," He recalled, "she reminded me of a little bird, hopping around and chirping. Joseph usually found some excuse to buy her a trinket."

"So did you, as I remember. You still spend more on the children than yourself. You should have kept some of that money you gave Elizabeth for a wedding gift."

"She and her husband are just starting out, and they needed it. Besides, what would I use it for? There's nothing I really need right now." Something He saw through the window caught His attention, and He jumped up from the table and ran to the window. "Joanna," He called, "get down off that wall. Now." He returned to His meal.

"Is that child climbing again?" Mary exclaimed in exasperation. "I don't think I'll ever be able to civilize her. She will never get a proper husband. Only an idiot would marry her." At the sound of a quarrelsome young male voice outside the window, she sighed. "I was enjoying the quiet. Who is that?"

Jesus smiled at her choice of words. "The--not my word--idiot who will marry her."

Mary walked to the window. "Thomas bar David! Oh no, Son! You have to be teasing."

"No, there is your future son-in-law, loud voice and all." Seeing her unhappy expression, He added comfortingly, "It will be all right, mother. Thomas is going to turn into a fine young man."

"If you say so. I know you can see the future," she said quietly. "You can read people's thoughts, too. Those abilities have grown stronger as you have grown older. And I know you can heal. When the children come to you with their little cuts and bruises, you let them think you are just comforting them or checking their injuries. But those injuries heal much too fast for it to be natural healing. Nothing dramatic enough to be called a miracle, and being children, they don't notice; but the power is there. You were always so quiet about it that I know you don't want anyone to find out. Why?"

"I don't want to draw undue attention to myself now. The time isn't right. If my enemies became aware of where I am, they would be on me. I can't lose time contending with them. I will only have three years to train the people who will carry out my work."

Mary finished the last stitch in Joanna's dress and folded it. "When we took you to the Temple as a baby to dedicate you to God, there was an old man there named Simeon. He said you would meet a lot of opposition someday, but I can't imagine you having any real enemies. Everyone who knows you likes and respects you. You're always willing to help the neighbors, and Levi says you're an even better craftsman than Joseph." She smiled at the resigned expression that suddenly appeared on her Son's face. "I can read your thoughts, too, Son, or at least your expression right now. That is your Aunt-Abigail-is-on-her-way expression."

"Mother, I love Abigail. She's sweet and kind and patient--"

"But she's an incurable matchmaker," she broke in.

"Well," He sighed, "at least this time she doesn't have some young lady in tow."

"Abigail's just proud of you, Son. She thinks you're wonderful, and so do I."

"She thinks I am her dead brother's son. You are my mother. Don't you think you two ladies are just a little biased?" He teased.

"Of course we're biased where you're concerned. But that doesn't mean we're mistaken." She began clearing the table. "Abigail thinks that with your intelligence and good reputation, you could even be on the Sanhedrin one day."

"I hate to disappoint you, but that is never going to happen."

"Then it's their loss, not yours."

CHAPTER THREE

In God's Stead

A SHORT, PLUMP WOMAN in a blue robe stepped through the open door. She hugged Jesus and Mary. "Mary, Deborah and I are going to Sepphoris tomorrow. We want to pick up some cloth. Do you want to go?"

"I'd like very much to go. Thank you for asking."

Abigail began pulling items from a cloth bag. "I have some things for the children." She drew out a small dress, a bracelet for Elizabeth, and several pairs of sandals.

"Abigail, that's very generous of you, but you're spoiling them, especially the younger ones."

Abigail dismissed Mary's objection with a wave of her hand. "Let me spoil them. I don't have any of my own." She handed Jesus a handsome blue and white prayer shawl. "I hope you like it, Jesus. Sometimes my weaving turns out fine, and sometimes it's not so fine."

"This turned out beautifully. Thank you. And I have something for you."

He went to the shop and returned with the wooden bowl.

Joanna's six-year-old playmate from across the street burst through the door. "Jesus, Joanna climbed a tree and can't get down. Can you come help her?"

"Jesus is tired, Tirzah," Mary explained. "Ask James to help her."

"I did. He said he was tired of her following him everywhere, and he was going to leave her up there an hour or so to teach her a lesson. Then he left, so I came to get Jesus."

"An hour or so!" Mary said, dismayed. "I don't know what to do with that boy anymore."

"I know what to do, mother." Jesus handed her the shawl. "Excuse me, ladies. I'll be back after I take care of Joanna--and James."

Tirzah took Jesus' larger hand in her small hand. "I'll show you where Joanna is. Do you want me to tell you where James went?"

"Yes, I really do want to talk to James," He answered as they walked out the door.

A broad smile spread across Abigail's round face. "I suspect that James will be the one looking for a tree to climb when Jesus catches up with him. You know, Mary, I was very concerned about the children when Joseph died. Jesus was barely sixteen, and Joanna was just a few weeks old, but He has done a wonderful job of raising the children. And you have, too, of course."

"Jesus deserves most of the credit. He really was my rock when Joseph died. I don't know how we would have survived that terrible time without Him. He has had so little time for Himself since then. He slips out before dawn or at night by Himself to pray." Mary laid the shawl on a bench. "I'm sorry, Abigail. Please sit down, and I'll get you a drink. When Tirzah came in, I forgot."

"Elizabeth told me she wants Jesus to build her house."

"He finished drawing the plans for it yesterday. I know she wants to leave her in-laws' house as soon as possible. They're nice to her, but it's not the same as having her own place."

"The addition He built for you was well planned and well built. He's very skilled. He gets more like His father every day."

"Yes," Mary agreed. "He's just like His Father."

"And He looks like Joseph, too, don't you think?"

"He's tall like Joseph was, and He has the same color hair. Another cup of water, Abigail?"

"No, thank you, dear. I have to leave." She stood up. "We'll come by for you early tomorrow."

Jesus walked through the door. "Well, mother, Joanna is safely back on solid ground."

"She was probably trying to catch that yellow bird she keeps talking about."

Abigail picked up the carved bowl Jesus had given her. "Mary, do you want to go with us to Jerusalem next week for the Passover? It would be safer if we all travel together. I don't like to take the main road all the way into the city, and some of those little side roads are dangerous, with bandits roaming them."

"Yes, I think we should go together. I don't like the main road, either. When the Romans have too many crucifixion victims to put them on Golgotha, they put the crosses beside the main highway to try to intimidate people into submission." Mary failed to notice that her

Son had become somberly quiet. "When Jesus was little, He and Joseph and I were coming home from Jerusalem. We didn't know the Romans made a practice of placing crosses along the road, and we walked right past them." She closed her eyes, trying to shut out the memory. "Sometimes I think I can still hear those men screaming. Most of all, I hated for Jesus to see something like that." She pushed it out of her thoughts. "It will be dark soon. Tell James to walk home with you."

"James is going to be busy for quite a while, mother," Jesus advised her. "Abigail, tell Judas I said to escort you home."

"Thank you. And thank you for the beautiful carved bowl. As you know, my husband can't even carve meat. Good night."

Abigail suppressed a smile as she walked by the corner of the house. James was stacking lumber in the back yard and grumbling to himself. She stopped to talk to her nephew.

"It's very nice of you to volunteer to help your brother, James. Jesus has a lot of responsibility, caring for His mother and His younger brothers and sisters."

"Yes, Aunt Abigail," James mumbled through clenched teeth.

Abigail heard him mutter something about "lord and master" and "bossy" as he moved a stack of boards.

Jesus sat back down at the table and rubbed His eyes. "Keep an eye on Joanna, mother. I found her crawling around the top of the hill this morning." He reached for the water pitcher and a cup. "I'm not going to let James go to Sepphoris again without someone older going with him. There's a lot of unrest under the surface in Galilee, and he's just the right age to do something foolish."

"Like what?"

"Get mixed up with the Zealots, or start a fight with the Roman soldiers."

"I'm surprised that the Zealots haven't tried to get you to join them."

"They did. I turned them down. I sympathize with their wanting to free Israel from Rome, but this is not the time or way to free Israel." Jesus laughed at the recollection of His discussion with the Zealots. "They ended up calling me a coward."

"I don't think that's funny," Mary said indignantly.

"You will one day, mother."

Mary noticed a coil of papers lying on a shelf just inside the shop door. She reached out and picked it up. "Is this the plans for Elizabeth's house?"

"No. It's the scroll Eleazar gave me."

Mary unrolled the parchment. "This passage is marked." She began reading from the psalm. "They pierced my hands and my feet." She looked up from the page. "Jesus, this sounds like crucifixion. Why did you mark this passage?"

Her Son's troubled face reinforced the cold fear the words of Psalm Twenty-two had stirred in her soul. "Son, answer me. Why are you reading this?"

"Mother," He answered reluctantly, "you know what Simeon told you at the Temple twenty-three years ago. You know why that psalm is marked. I would spare you that grief if I could, but I can't." Anticipating her reaction, He moved quickly around the table and took her in His arms, pressing her face gently against His chest to muffle her scream. "I'm sorry for what you're going to go through. I've made my peace with my fate, and that's what you have to do, too. You have to accept it."

The sobs wracking her body nearly engulfed her words. "No! I don't have to accept it, and neither do you. There's no reason for you to be treated like that."

Suddenly becoming aware of someone approaching, He tried again to calm her. "Mother, please listen to me."

"No! You listen to me." Tears streaked the tortured face looking up at Him. "All the chances Joseph and I took to protect you, and all the years we were allowed to raise and love you." She almost choked on her next words. "Now you're telling me that it was all for nothing--that you're going to die that terrible death, and there's nothing I can do about it."

Over Mary's head Jesus saw Abigail standing in the doorway. She had heard the last thing Mary had said, and she stood stunned, her face registering unspeakable shock.

Mary leaned her head against her Son's chest, too emotionally drained to care about the interruption.

Abigail finally found her voice. "I'm sorry...I didn't know...I didn't mean to intrude...I forgot my scarf," she stammered in confusion.

"It's all right, Abigail," He said softly. "Come in." He brushed the tears from His mother's face. "In spite of what you just heard, I'm not going to die anytime soon."

"I don't know what this is all about, Jesus, but I won't add to the load you're already carrying. I will keep what I've heard to myself."

"Thank you. I know you will. And I would tell you if I could."

"You probably think I'm a talkative woman, but I'm very careful what I talk about."

"Why don't I tell you what I really think of you, so you won't have to wonder about it?"

She nodded. "I might as well know."

"Except for my parents, all my life you have given me more love and support than anyone else. And I love you dearly."

"Coming from you, that means more to me than you know." Abigail forced a tired smile. She picked up her scarf from a bench. "I'll close the door on my way out."

She left, pulling the front door closed. The closed front door, a commonly understood sign that a family did not want visitors, would give Jesus and His mother some desperately needed time to try to solve whatever problem was tormenting them.

CHAPTER FOUR

The Lamb

JESUS, HIS EYES BLURRED BY TEARS, looked down at His mother. He felt tired with a weariness that did not come from the long hours of working in the shop.

"Mother, sit down. Let me explain. You need to try to understand." He pulled out a chair for her and sat down facing her, keeping her hands covered with His own. "You remember the angel told Joseph, when he told him my name, that I would save my people from their sins. You're familiar with the sacrificial system, and you understand that God's forgiveness comes only by the death of a sacrificial lamb. The people have come to the point where the Temple sacrifices are routine, and mean nothing to them." Jesus wiped the tears from His own eyes. "My Father plans to replace the Temple sacrifices with one final sacrifice, and He will provide the lamb Himself. I was sent down here to be that sacrifice."

Mary's sobs had ceased, ended by exhaustion. "How can He do this to His own Son? If He really tries, He can find another way. I know He can."

"He tried for hundreds of years, with the law and the prophets and the sacrificial system. Before I left Heaven, He even tried to find a way that He could come Himself and spare me, but there was no other way. I'm all He has left to try."

"I don't care about any of that. I don't want my Son tortured to death."

"Yes, you do care, mother." He handed her a cup of water. "Do you remember finding a butterfly struggling in a spider's web last summer? It wasn't even a pretty butterfly, just a pathetic-looking little thing all bedraggled from trying to escape; but you freed it. You couldn't stand to see even an insect die in a trap like that."

"Freeing that butterfly didn't cost me my Son."

"But people are worth so much more. Can't you see that my Father is in the same position, wanting to free the human race from Satan's web?"

Mary remained quiet for a moment, trying to keep His words from taking hold. As if by denying His fate, she could wish it away. "There are other ways to help," she pleaded when she spoke again. "With your talent for healing, you could be a fine physician. You could spend your whole life relieving suffering. Or you could someday teach God's truth from the bench of the Sanhedrin. That matters most to God, doesn't it-- teaching His law?"

"Yes, but His law is fulfilled in His Son." He smoothed the lines of grief from her forehead. "All those wonderful things you and Abigail want for me, I know you want them because you love me; and I love you both for that. But it can't be. My life is set on a course mapped out by God, and with His help I'll follow it to its end."

"Do you know"--she hesitated, then forced herself to ask--"how long you can stay with us?"

"I know, but if I told you, all you would see ahead of you from now on would be that day. It's better that you go on with your life as normally as possible. I want you to go to Sepphoris with Abigail and Deborah tomorrow. Even if you can't really enjoy the trip, it's one small way of learning to make the most of each day."

"How long have you known? You knew who you were at twelve years old, but how long have you known about this?"

"I was about ten when we began studying the text in Isaiah about the Suffering Servant. Then I started going through other prophecies. I knew I had been born in Bethlehem, and Joseph had told me about the star and the angels."

"And all this time, you kept working and raising the children.   I underestimated you, Son. But you're wrong about this," she argued, grasping at any hope that crossed her mind. "You won't have to go through all that suffering. It will just be a test of obedience for you, like it was for Abraham, when God asked for Isaac's life."

"Mother, don't give death credit for too much power. Death is under God's control, like everything else. Do you remember the passage from the Psalms that I told you to hold on to when Joseph died--the one that says weeping endures for the night, but joy comes in the morning? That's the way it will be when I die. Just a matter of a few hours, and I'll rise from the dead. I promise you that." Jesus poured water into a bowl, dipped a cloth in the water and dabbed carefully at

Mary's eyes. "You don't want the children to see you with your eyes red and swollen. It would upset them."

"I just can't make myself believe God will let that happen to you."

"Don't blame Him, mother. He didn't create all this sin and turmoil." He set the bowl and cloth aside. "Over the last few years, I've remembered more and more of Heaven, and what happened there when I left. My Father was standing by the door, holding me and grieving as if I were already dead. I never saw Him cry like that before. When I was small, I had a few years when I didn't know what would happen to me, but He never had that luxury." He leaned over and kissed her. "It's getting dark. I'll go bring the children home. The crowds are beginning to gather in this area for Passover, and so are the criminals who will prey on them."

Jesus left, and Mary wearily leaned her arms on the table, cradling her head in her hands. She had to smile as she heard His voice through the window, telling James there would be enough daylight left for another half an hour of work. He also directed the disgruntled teenager to be in the shop early the next morning.

Working numbly, she began unrolling sleeping mats for the children. Jesus was right about trying to make the most of each day. One of the best ways to do that was to maintain her usual routine.

Mary was used to her Son being consistently right, but He had to be wrong about the Crucifixion. Crucifixion was a Roman punishment, and He had never had any conflict with Roman authorities. He had spent a lot of time and effort teaching all the children respect for both religious and civil law.

She put the dress Abigail had brought Joanna in a chest with Joanna's other clothes, and laid Elizabeth's bracelet on a shelf.

Jesus returned with Joses and Simon trailing Him. Joanna was riding on His shoulders. He bent down to keep Joanna from hitting her head on the door. "Judas should be here in a few minutes, mother."

James, wearing a disgusted expression, appeared in the doorway. "It's too dark to work anymore."

"You're right, James," the head of the household agreed. "You can start again tomorrow morning."

Judas straggled in to make the count complete. Jesus gave His brothers and sister time to fall asleep, then picked up the prayer shawl Abigail had given Him and slipped out of the house. Mary had regained her composure, and she managed a smile for Him as He left.

Jesus walked a few yards down the street, then turned off the street to climb a hill overlooking the village. Ariel and Tobias, the two angels God had charged with protecting His Son, accompanied their Prince. Jesus settled Himself under a tree. The children's dog had followed Him. Dogs were not popular animals with the Jews, but Jesus had allowed the children to keep the stray. Ahab nestled next to Him and laid his head on His lap.

"Did I tell you to follow me?" Jesus asked with mock severity. Ahab whined an apology, and Jesus reached over and stroked the dog's yellow head. "It's all right. You obey better than the children do."

Jesus leaned His head back against the tree and pulled the prayer shawl onto His head. He stared up at the star-sprinkled sky, looking toward the North, looking toward Home.

"Good evening, Father. Thank you for your help today, especially for protecting Joanna. I know Satan knows where I am, and I know you're holding him back from a direct attack on me. I'm grateful for that, but now he has decided to attack me through the children. That yellow bird Joanna keeps chasing doesn't exist. It's a lure he's using to draw her into danger. He will be stalking all the children like a hungry wolf, trying to wear me down."

He remained quiet for a while, letting the soundless voice of His Father drift down into His soul like a cool, refreshing rain.

"Father, thank you for giving me a carpenter for my foster father. Growing up learning that craft helped me remember all the times you and I spent building things together, though we built on a much greater scale."

Ahab whined and moved restlessly in his sleep. Jesus stroked the dog comfortingly. "I miss seeing you and Michael and Gabriel and everyone else, Father. I know you're all near me, but I miss talking with you face to face. The longer I stay in this world, the more I feel like a stranger in a strange land."

A light breeze began stirring, wafting away the physical weariness. "Mother is unhappy because she thinks I'm working too much, but I only have seven years left in Nazareth, and I want to leave her and the children as financially secure as I can. And building things reminds me of Home, and keeps me from thinking too much about the cross. Mother doesn't want to think about it, either; so she will convince herself that I'm mistaken, because that is what she wants to believe."

Jesus smiled wryly. "Seven years to turn James into a responsible adult. Parting the Red Sea was easier. Elizabeth wants me to mediate every disagreement between her and her new husband; Simon believes in solving every problem with his fists; and Joanna seems bent on exterminating herself. She needs an extra guardian angel. The one caring for her now is overworked."

He looked down at the village. All the lamps had been extinguished, except the one His mother had left burning for Him. He could not see it from here, but it was always there until He returned. The darkness was profound, but the stars, looking close enough to touch, made the night seem friendly.

"Abba," He said, using the intimate, small child's word for an earthly father, "you told me I could come Home whenever I chose--without penalty, and you would think no less of me. Leaving would be the safest thing for me. One wrong act of any kind on my part, and there is no one to redeem me. But there is much more at risk than my own safety." He drew the shawl closer around His shoulders. "I was so involved in settling one of Simon's disputes the other day, that I almost considered not taking time to return that accidental overpayment Levi left with James. I would not have kept his money, but I had promised Levi I would return it that day. It might seem a small thing to some people, but I would have been breaking my word. Lying, in effect. Only a perfect sacrifice is acceptable to you, and that perfection would have been gone. Satan will be throwing much worse obstacles than that in my path as I move closer to the cross. Please stay close to me."

Jesus rose to leave. Ahab climbed to his feet to follow Him. The dog took a few steps and stopped. He stood rooted to the ground, the hair on his neck bristling, snarling at something hiding in the darkness. Jesus' invisible protectors moved to either side of Him. Jesus reached down and put His hand on the dog's shoulders.

"I know he's out there, Ahab." He gazed intently into the darkness, sorting out shapes and shadows. One shadow was darker than the others. "Angry because my Father would not let you listen, Satan? You lured Joanna to that hill. You're a coward, and killing children is the extent of your courage. Get out."

At Jesus' command the darker shadow vanished with a suddenness that startled Ahab. The dog responded to the disappearance with a surprised yelp.

"He will be back, unfortunately. Let's go home."

Ahab trailed Jesus down the hill and along the street home. Instead of begging to be allowed inside with the children, as he usually did, the dog stationed himself outside the front door. He looked up at the hilltop and growled before drifting into a fitful sleep. The guardian angels took up sentry positions above either side of the house, hovering there, as they always did.

CHAPTER FIVE

The Joy of His Way

THE SOUND OF HAMMERS coming from the shop woke Mary. Worn out by emotional turmoil, she had fallen asleep sitting on a bench in the kitchen, her back against a wall. Jesus had spread the prayer shawl over her to keep away the chill of the spring night.

Judging from the stack of dishes, He had given the children breakfast. He must have told them to be quiet and eat in another room so they would not awaken her. He had also set them at their assigned tasks. Joanna was carrying water out the door for Ahab, and Judas was clearing scrap lumber from the back yard. Except for James, the boys would go next to classes at the synagogue school. After classes Jesus usually allowed those who had finished their chores to spend the rest of the day however they wished.

Mary could imagine the conversation between the two brothers as they worked in the shop. She had heard it often. James would be sullenly following Jesus' instructions. Jesus would be patiently explaining that He could not be in Nazareth always, and James must be prepared to accept responsibility for the family.

Joanna returned to the kitchen for a bowl of scraps for Ahab. She was not allowed to attend the synagogue school, although she went to the synagogue itself with Mary. Jesus always took at least an hour every day to educate His little sister Himself at home. It was a practice He had begun when Elizabeth was Joanna's age.

Noticing Elizabeth's disappointment when she had not been allowed to follow her adored big brother to school, Jesus had approached the rabbi and respectfully requested that she be allowed to attend the school. The rabbi, loudly stubborn, had spluttered that he could not tolerate such a break with tradition. Jesus, quietly determined, had come home and set about sharing His synagogue training with His younger sister. When the teacher had found out that his best pupil had outwitted him, he protested to Joseph that educating Elizabeth was a mistake. The strong-willed little girl would misuse her learning. And besides, the mother-daughter oral teaching tradition was good enough for her. Joseph, squarely behind his foster Son, gently hinted that if the teacher gave Jesus any trouble, the rabbi's eagerly awaited addition to his house would go to the end of the carpenter's list of priorities. The matter was dropped.

Mary began rolling up sleeping mats and rinsing dishes. By the time Abigail and Elizabeth's friend Deborah arrived, the house was neat again.

Deborah, agonizingly shy and bordering on plain, was a year younger than nineteen-year-old Elizabeth. She had warmed to Elizabeth's friendly manner, even though she sometimes felt overshadowed by Mary's pretty, outgoing daughter. Elizabeth and Jesus were two of the few people she could talk to with ease.

Mary took a woven bag from a peg in the kitchen. "Deborah, would you tell Jesus we're leaving now and taking Joanna with us? That will give Him some relief from chasing her. She can have her lessons when she gets back. He's in the shop. I'll get Joanna."

Deborah opened the shop door for James, who was carrying a small stack of boards, and spoke to Jesus. "Good morning, Jesus."

He looked up from the assortment of tools on the table. "Good morning, Deborah."

"Your mother is going to take Joanna with us. She said that way you won't have to chase her all day."

"Thank you. Tell mother I'm deeply grateful. That is the most active child I've ever seen."

"Since we're leaving so early, we should easily be back before sunset."

"If you let Aunt Abigail haggle with all those merchants, you won't be home by sun*rise*. Please try to keep her out of a few of the bazaars."

"I'll do my best. I saw two Roman patrols marching toward Sepphoris this morning. They must be searching for someone. I don't like the Romans any better than any other Nazarene, but they do give us a measure of safety along the roads."

"Deborah, come on, dear," Mary's voice called through the window.

Deborah joined Mary, Abigail, and Joanna. The four of them walked down the street toward the Sepphoris road.

James sawed and chiseled under Jesus' supervision. Because Jesus had told him that the quality of his work would determine how many hours he would work tomorrow, James took extra care in his efforts.

The two of them stopped for lunch, abandoning the confining walls of the shop to eat under an olive tree in the back yard. Jesus tried to start a conversation with James, but the teenager declined to talk. James obviously resented having a man who was not his father in authority over him; but he usually, although grudgingly, treated Jesus with the respect their culture required be accorded an eldest son.

James tossed the few remnants of his lunch to Ahab, and they went back to work. As the afternoon was drawing to a close, James asked Jesus to inspect his work.

Jesus ran His hands over a table and a bench. "Very good work, James. The lines are straight, and the joints are solidly put together."

James beamed at the praise. "I'm not as good as you, or as good as father was. Thomas' father said I never will be, but if you think I have some skill, maybe I can learn."

"Thomas' father is mistaken. You have the basic ability. If you are willing to pay the price of honing that ability, you can be excellent. I think you've done enough for today. Quit if you wish."

James was out the door before Jesus had finished speaking. He almost collided with Elizabeth, who was carrying a large basket.

Elizabeth set the basket on the floor in a corner of the shop. "Is mother home, Jesus?"

"No. She and Abigail and Deborah went to Sepphoris. They should be home soon."

"If she isn't home by the time I leave, tell her I returned her basket." She reached into the basket and took out a pomegranate. "I got these at the market this morning and brought mother some. Want one?"

"Thank you, but not right now." He moved some tools from the bench to clear a seat for her. "I'm glad you came by. I haven't seen you for a while."

Elizabeth was closest to Him in age. Because the two of them had struggled together to care for the younger children after Joseph's death, she had also become His closest sibling emotionally. Curious about everything and highly intelligent, Elizabeth sometimes chafed under the restraints on women in her culture.

She moved over to make a place for Him on the bench. "Sit down and talk to me."

"I promised I would finish this chair today, but we can talk while I work."

"Don't you ever stop working?"

"Work isn't just a necessity to me. I enjoy making things."

"It's a good thing you enjoy it. You never had much time for yourself. You inherited all six of us little responsibilities at once when father died. Sometimes I feel bad that we consumed so much of your life."

He smiled at her from across the room. "Next to God, my family is the most important thing in my life." He picked up three huge nails from a box. "Don't ever think any of you were just responsibilities. You were also a joy to me. Seeing the way all of you have turned out has been rewarding."

"Until James and Judas got old enough to think they know it all?"

"They will outgrow that, in time."

"You know, Micah really admires you for your endurance and determination," she said, referring to her husband. "He says you're tougher than nails."

Jesus looked down at the three spikes in His hands. "I hope so," He said, almost to Himself. "Everything depends on it."

Elizabeth, wanting to draw His attention back to visiting with her, decided teasing Him was the quickest way to accomplish that goal. He always joined in, tolerated, or ignored her teasing, depending on how busy He was.

"Someone else admires you, too."

"Oh? Who?" He asked absently.

"Deborah and Naomi."

"They're your best friends, so I make an extra effort to make them welcome when they visit mother."

"Apparently you succeeded beautifully, because they both think you're kind and attractive. And you're too intelligent to believe they're interested in visiting that often with mother, who is twenty years older."

"Elizabeth, if you have set your head on matchmaking, you can forget about it." He began rummaging through the toolbox. "I don't have time for your nonsense. Counting mother and Abigail, I have about a dozen ladies in my life already. I don't need any more."

"Mother and Abigail are only two."

He leaned over to look her directly in the eye. "You and Joanna account for at least ten more. Don't you have places to go and people to annoy, Little Sister?"

"I would rather annoy you, Big Brother."

"I'm honored," He said drily. "Elizabeth, I love you, and I don't want you to take this the wrong way, but please go home."

"I can't. Micah is repairing something or other, and he doesn't want me trying to supervise. He told me not to come back for at least two hours."

"Your husband chased you out of your house, and your brother is about ready to chase you out of His. Doesn't that suggest something to you?"

"Yes. It suggests that everybody I meet today is going to be ill-humored."

Jesus laid down a chisel and sat down beside her. "I'm not being ill-humored with you. I'm trying to explain that you can't make that decision for me. Don't you care what I think?"

"Of course I care. You and Micah are the two most important men in my life."

"My sympathies to Micah. Can we please agree that you won't do any more matchmaking, at least not for me?"

"Fine, Your Royal Highness," she answered haughtily. "If you don't like my friends, find your own bride."

"Your friends are both very sweet young ladies. But my Father chose my bride for me many years ago, and that choice can't be changed."

Elizabeth's mouth dropped open in astonishment. "I had no idea father had made a covenant for you. He and mother never mentioned it. I'm sorry. I didn't mean to interfere."

"You just want me to be happy, and I appreciate that."

"Who is she?"

"You would think I was teasing if I told you, so it won't do you any good to ask."

"Mother will tell me. She would have signed the covenant."

"Mother did not sign any covenant. Elizabeth, do you consider it your duty in life to exasperate me?"

She smiled sweetly. "No. I consider it a pleasure."

Jesus returned to carving the chair. "If you can't go home, please go visit Naomi."

An idea presented itself to her. "If you or the bride changes your mind, Deborah or Naomi--"

"Madam, you have just used up my last shred of patience."

Son of My Love

He set the knife aside and stepped around the worktable. Picking up His dumbfounded sister from the bench, He carried her outside and set her sandaled feet gently on the doorstep. "Thank you for the pomegranates. Come back when you want to visit instead of investigate. Good afternoon, Madam Micah bar Jonah. I'm sure Naomi will be delighted to see you."

He closed the door and latched it. Speechless for one of the few times in her life, Elizabeth stared at the closed door. She considered going around to the front door, then decided against it. Her brother was very efficient. He was probably already closing that door, too.

She recovered her voice. "I'll find out," she sang out through the window.

Facing the boring prospect of more than an hour with nothing to do, she decided to follow His suggestion and visit Naomi.

Jesus immersed Himself in the carving, working happily until He heard His mother knock on the door. He lifted the latch. Mary walked in, a baffled expression on her face.

"Son, why did you lock me out of the house?"

"I locked Elizabeth out, and left the door locked to discourage her from coming back. I don't mind her teasing, but I have to deter her matchmaking some way."

She laughed at her Son's matter-of-fact way of dealing with the sister problem. "I'm glad you two love each other. I can't imagine how you would get along if you disliked each other."

CHAPTER SIX

The Galilee Road

IT WAS TIME TO LEAVE NAZARETH. Over the last seven years, Jesus had trained James and His other three brothers to provide for themselves and their mother. They were now able to shoulder those responsibilities, which had once been His. He could move on to the duty God had assigned to Him alone.

Jesus set the toolbox on a shelf at the end of the day and looked around at the shop for the last time. The tools too large for the box were in order on the wall, and the floor was swept clean of sawdust.

"Hello, Uncle Jesus," a small voice lisped.

He turned to see Ruth, Elizabeth's three-year-old, smiling up at Him from the doorway. Elizabeth was holding her month-old son. Ruth ran to His arms, and He picked her up.

"Hello, Ruth. Thank you for coming to visit me."

"We came to say goodbye. I don't want you to go," she blurted out.

"I'll be back to see you."

Elizabeth shifted Daniel to her other shoulder to rest her arm. "The shop looks neat and orderly, but then it always did when you were in charge."

"Everything has been taken care of. I signed the property over to James, and the taxes are paid for the rest of the year."

"You know, of course, that this place will only look this neat for about two days."

"I'm sure of it. James has developed into a good carpenter, but neatness is not one of his traits."

"You will probably have to come back just to straighten out the chaos." She reached out and took His hand. "So why go? No one wants you to leave."

"I have to, Elizabeth. It's what I was born for."

"I couldn't stand to be here tomorrow to watch you walk away." She blinked back the tears that were on the verge of spilling over. "But I couldn't let you leave without making sure you knew how much Micah and I appreciate all you've done for us." She lost her struggle with her tears. "And how very much we love you."

"Micah was here this morning. Thank you both for the gift. Elizabeth, you and Micah probably need--"

She interrupted His intended offer. "Don't you dare try to return that money because you think we need it more. Or for any other reason, Big Brother."

The neighbors' children had begun a noisy game, and their shouting was beginning to overwhelm Jesus and Elizabeth's conversation. He reached over and lifted Daniel from her arms. "We can't talk here. Let's walk back to your house. I'll carry the baby for you."

She laughed, in spite of her sadness, as her memory brought back a long-forgotten incident. "Are you throwing me out of the house again?"

"I didn't throw you out," He said with obviously pretended indignation as He opened the door for her. "I very gently carried you out."

"I stand corrected, Sir." She took Ruth's hand. "I was evicted, as I recall, because I was being nosy and a matchmaker. At the same time. It took me a while, but I finally concluded that you would tell me about the bride when you wanted me to know."

"Let's take the path behind the houses instead of the street. It will be quieter there."

They walked slowly so Ruth could keep up with them. Daniel fell asleep on Jesus' shoulder.

The breeze blew a strand of blue-black hair across Elizabeth's face, and she brushed it aside. "Micah told me people were coming into the shop to say goodbye when he was there this morning."

"People have been stopping by all week."

"Mother said you are planning to stay in Capernaum."

"For a while. I will be doing a lot of traveling."

"What will you be doing?"

"Teaching, mostly."

"I suppose there's a little selfishness in my wanting to keep you here. I want my children to have the benefit of having you in their lives like I did."

"You and Micah can pass on the training I gave you to your children. You're both very capable."

"Speaking of passing on training, I don't think I ever thanked you for educating me. I can already see how that is benefiting Ruth. You took a risk in going against the rabbi. He could have made a lot of trouble for you."

"Fortunately, Joseph was the only good carpenter in Nazareth. And the rabbi wanted that addition to his house very badly."

They both laughed. She stopped laughing and looked up at Him.

"Jesus, why did you call him 'Joseph?' I don't ever remember you calling him 'father.' You always called him 'sir.'"

He stopped and turned to face her. "Let's sit down. I want to talk to you."

She found a seat on a rock. Holding Daniel carefully, He lowered Himself to the ground.

"Elizabeth, you told me once that there was something a little mysterious about me, like I knew something I wasn't telling you. It wasn't that I wanted to shut you out. The time was not right to tell you. But starting tomorrow, I will be trying to tell everyone all about myself, so this is the right time." He held her hand in a firm grasp, steadying her against the shock He knew His words would bring. "I loved Joseph, and he loved me, but he was not my father."

She sat statue still for a moment. "Our parents adopted you?" she finally managed to ask.

"No. Mother is my birth mother. Joseph raised me as his son."

Her voice was little more than a whisper. "But you're so much like him--the way you talk, and your gestures. I never would have guessed you were not related."

"I picked up many of his habits when I was small, and they have stayed with me."

She smiled at Him as the shock began to wear off. "I don't care who you are. You provided for us, and kept us together as a family when our relatives wanted to take us and raise us separately." A scowl crossed her face. "But it makes me angry that mother would keep something like this from me. It makes me wonder what else I don't know."

"Mother isn't keeping anything else from you. She and Joseph kept all the stories about my birth to themselves because they didn't know what else to do. Mother's cousin Elizabeth and her husband and son knew."

"Do you know who your father is?"

"I talk to Him all the time." Ruth climbed onto His lap. He put His arm around His niece. "Elizabeth, I'm asking you to remember you have said more than once that I'm the steadiest, most reliable person you've ever known; because what I'm going to tell you will sound completely unbelievable. It's going to test your faith in my character. But it's the truth."

"You've never lied to me. I don't think you would start now."

"You know Israel is waiting for their Messiah. The wait is over. I stayed here to take care of mother and the children until James matured enough to take over that responsibility. My Father is God, the God of Abraham, Isaac, and Jacob. He sent me here, and He will take me Home when this mission is over."

Her face went totally blank. "What?" she gasped. "Did I hear you right?"

He smiled. "What did you hear me say?"

"That you're the Messiah. You're not teasing me again?"

"I'm as serious as I've ever been."

"But why would God send His Son to Nazareth. With this town's reputation?"

"Because He wanted people to know that no one is too lowly to be redeemed. That His kingdom is open to anyone who wants to enter."

Ruth yawned and nestled her nodding head on her uncle's shoulder. Jesus held her closer so she would not tumble out of His arm.

Elizabeth looked at her brother. Daniel was asleep on one of His shoulders, and Ruth on the other. *How typical*, she thought. *He was always carrying or sheltering one of us.*

"I believe you, Jesus. I don't know if the rest of the family will, but I do. And not just because you're my brother. I've watched you all my life, and I know your integrity. Like you said, father was the only good carpenter in Nazareth; and after you grew up, you were. That put you both in a position where you could have overcharged and gouged people, but neither of you ever did. And it must have been tempting sometimes, with such a large family to support."

"It means a lot to me to know that at least one person in the family believes in me. This is going to be a long, lonely journey for me."

"Mother and Abigail have always had a lot of confidence in you."

"They're going to need all the confidence they can muster before this is over."

She reached for Ruth. "Holding both of them must be tiring. I don't want to wake Daniel, but I'll take Ruth."

He shook His head. "I will only get to see them three more times. I want to hold them as long as I can."

Not wanting His last day at home to be completely somber, she tried to lighten the mood. "You have to be divine. You're the only person I know who can make me speechless occasionally. At least when I was left standing there with my mouth open, I wasn't saying or doing something to embarrass you."

"You never embarrassed me. You drove me nearly to total exasperation sometimes, but you never embarrassed me. I've always been proud of you."

"Do James and the others know who you are?"

"I'll talk to Joanna this evening. She's fourteen now, so she will be able to understand. I'm not going to discuss it with James or the other three boys. It will be years before they will be willing to even listen to anything I say, much less believe me."

"The boys are jealous of you, but Joanna adores you. She would walk through fire for you."

"We should go. You need to get home." Still holding Ruth and Daniel, He stood to His feet. They resumed their walk along the winding dirt path. "Elizabeth, there is a captain at the Roman garrison near here. His name is Lucius. I met him in Sepphoris, and we became friends. He's a good man, disciplined and professional. When he heard I was leaving, he told me that if anyone in my family ever needed help, to come to him."

"If the Nazarenes had known you were friends with a Roman officer, you might not have gotten out of Nazareth alive."

They could hear the voices of the people in the streets as they walked. Jesus heard Abigail call out to her husband. A twinge of homesickness for the town He had not yet left began tugging at Him.

"Jesus, be careful," Elizabeth said suddenly. "I overhear stories in the bazaars in Sepphoris. I know I'm not supposed to criticize the high priest, but Caiaphas is ruthless when it comes to protecting his power. If what you want to teach doesn't meet with his approval, he could be a real danger to you."

"I don't want you to distress yourself worrying about me, Elizabeth. I can protect myself--when I choose to."

Jesus carried the sleeping children inside and laid them on a mat. Elizabeth lit a lamp and set it on a shelf.

She invited Jesus to stay and talk, hoping to keep her brother with her a while longer.

"I have to leave now, Elizabeth. Tell Micah and Ruth goodbye for me."

With a final embrace and kiss for Elizabeth, He was gone, leaving by way of the street instead of the path. He walked at an unhurried pace along the nearly deserted street, as if trying to gather and store up His last few hours in Nazareth.

Micah spoke from behind her. "I'm sorry I missed seeing Jesus again, but I didn't know He was coming here."

"We came back here because it was too noisy to talk at His house." She corrected herself. "It isn't His house now." She leaned her head against the doorframe. "I went over there today because I didn't want to see Him leave tomorrow, but I had to watch Him walk away anyway. They're going to kill Him, Micah. I can sense it. Caiaphas and his hirelings will kill Him."

Micah slipped his arm around her shoulders. "Perhaps the Romans can protect Him. Pilate despises Caiaphas."

Elizabeth bit her lower lip to stop its trembling. "No. Caiaphas is devious enough to get whatever he wants.

And he wants to get rid of anyone he considers a threat to him."

"Jesus said the strangest thing when I was in the shop this morning. Levi was there with his son, and Levi remarked about how much he loved the boy. After Levi left, Jesus said, 'People talk about love like they know what it is.' But it was as if He was really talking to someone else instead of me."

CHAPTER SEVEN

Kingdom Come

THE SMOOTH SURFACE of the Sea of Galilee rippled as the fishing boat with thirteen very tired men aboard moved toward the other shore. On each side of the boat, two watchful presences kept their steadying hands on the craft. Unheard and unseen by the passengers, Jesus' protective angels talked about the week's happenings.

"It's about time the Prince got some rest," Ariel remarked. "He didn't even have time for a meal yesterday, and that crowd would have crushed Him if we had not been able to get the door closed. I know He wants to help people, but He is putting Himself in danger. Even with all His power, when He is this tired, the exhaustion could make Him slow to react and place Him in jeopardy."

The wind rose a little. Tobias took a firmer grip on the side of the boat. "At least out here He's safe. We don't have to worry about someone slipping through the crowd and attacking Him."

The object of their watch care slept in the stern. Jesus had spent many hours and vast energy on the crowds who had sought Him out everywhere He had gone. Tomorrow would bring more lame, blind, diseased, and demon-possessed, hundreds of them, in a desperate search for the help that no one else had been able to give. Unwilling to turn anyone away, He would slip out alone before dawn for prayer, then embark on the long days. The joy He saw in the faces of those liberated from pain and physical impairments always buoyed Him when the days became grueling.

The sudden, violent winds that the surrounding hills channeled down onto the smooth surface of the lake unexpectedly slammed against the boat and churned the placid waters into a raging gale. Huge waves spilled into the boat, threatening to swamp it.

Son of My Love

Tobias and Ariel seized the sides of the boat with both hands, clinging to it with all the strength they possessed.

Roaring winds and pounding waves sent the disciples stumbling toward the stern. The frightened men shook the sleeping Jesus. "Master, save us! Don't you care that we're all going to die?"

Jesus climbed to His feet and spoke to the shrieking storm. "Hush now! Calm down."

The disciples gaped in slack-jawed wonder as the wind, like a rowdy child embarrassed by a parental scolding, promptly settled into obedient silence. The surface of the lake was restored to its earlier calm.

"Why are you so afraid," He asked the twelve drenched and trembling men, "and why do you have so little faith in me?"

Jesus returned to His pillow in the stern, and the stunned disciples began whispering among themselves.

"What kind of man is this? Even the wind and the sea obey Him."

They looked at the exhausted Nazarene Carpenter beginning to drift back into sleep in the now steady boat. For the first time, they felt fear mingle with their respect for the power of this gentle, fascinating man.

"They didn't have to awaken Him," Ariel grumbled to Tobias. "This boat isn't going down as long as the Prince is on it. Near Him is the safest place they can be. You'd think they would know that by now."

Tobias relaxed his grip on the boat slightly. "I can't imagine why He chose these twelve. Apparently He sees something in them that we don't."

The calm lake gave the vessel a peaceful voyage the rest of the way. When the boat nudged against the shore, Jesus stepped out on the bank.

"I don't like the looks of this place," Ariel said nervously. "Something isn't right. It's too deserted. Even at this time of day, as close as we are to the lake, someone should be here on the shore—at least a few fishermen. That herd of pigs and a few herdsmen on that far hill over there are the only living things I see."

Tobias looked up at the top of the little hill near them that sloped down to the water. "That cemetery up there could be hiding criminals. Don't move one step away from the Prince."

Ariel and Tobias heard the screaming fury before the disciples heard, and moved between Jesus and the two onrushing creatures who had appeared from out of the graveyard. When the two drew closer, the disciples and the angels could see that the two wild-looking beings were actually men.

To Ariel and Tobias' dismay, Jesus stepped around the angels to confront the raving men. He held His arms out from His sides to keep Ariel and Tobias separated from the strangers from the tombs. The disciples, unable to see the angels, interpreted Jesus' movements as a signal for them to stand back. They waited uneasily, uncertain about the dangerous situation, as the men closed the distance between themselves and Jesus.

"Come out!" Jesus commanded.

The two strangers fell on their knees. The voices, deep and terrible, that rose from their throats, were not their own. "Jesus, Son of the Most High God, leave us alone," the devils infesting the men begged. "What do we have in common with you? Are you here to torment us even before the Judgment?"

Jesus looked at the wretched men, with their wrists scarred by broken chains. The demons had driven them many times into the desert, and their sun-scorched skin added to their suffering. Through the babbling of the demons, Jesus heard the men's silent heart cry, and saw it reflected in their eyes.

"Come out of these men, you unclean spirits," Jesus ordered. "What is your name?" He demanded of the devil that was speaking for the others.

"Legion," the demon answered, "for there are many of us."

Fearing imprisonment in Satan's Abyss more than anything else, the demons began pleading with Jesus. "Please, Lord, don't order us into the pit. Let us go into those pigs."

"Go!" Jesus answered.

The invisible beings tormenting the men fled the bodies of their hosts, leaving them limp on the ground where they had been kneeling. Jesus reached down and lifted them to their feet.

The pigs, feeding quietly on the hillside, suddenly started squealing frantically as the army of demons invaded their bodies. Unable to dislodge the devils, they began running wildly, trying to escape to the peace they had known only minutes before. In their panic they rushed headlong down the hill and plunged into the lake. Their thrashing around in the water soon ended, and the waters of the lake were still again.

The herdsmen fled, running for the nearby town and carrying the story with them. In the hush on the shore, the disciples and the liberated demoniacs stared at the peaceful lake.

"They're dead; they're really gone," one of the freed men said to the other.

"They're gone," the other answered. "They won't bother us anymore, but they're not dead. Spirits don't die. God can destroy them if He chooses, but they don't die, as men die."

Jesus and the disciples, along with the two men He had set free, rested on the bank for a while. Jesus looked up when He heard the sound of voices. The herdsmen who had gone into town were running back to the lake, leading a crowd of townspeople toward Jesus. Even at a distance, Tobias and Ariel could hear the anger in their voices. The crowd began counting up the lost profits from their illegal enterprise. Those profits, undoubtedly at the bottom of the lake and definitely out of their reach, fueled their anger. They were muttering to each other about their misfortune. Jesus' two uneasy bodyguards quietly stationed themselves between their Prince and the approaching mob.

One of the rescued demoniacs was sitting on the bank, near Jesus. As the crowd drew closer, one person in the crowd, then another and another, recognized the healed man. Their angry march came to an abrupt halt. This rational, clear-thinking, sensibly clothed person was the same man who until about an hour ago had, along with his fellow sufferer, made the area too dangerous to travel. The people of the town had taken long detours to avoid walking past this place. The only residents who had used this land were the swine herdsmen, and they had been careful to stay on the opposite hill, keeping distance between themselves and the demon-possessed men.

The herdsmen had been too far away to clearly see the healing, but they had heard the demons' pleas to be allowed to enter the swine, followed by the praises of the freed men.

The crowd stared at the stranger who appeared to be the leader and healer. Any man who could control and change the behavior of someone so demon possessed had the kind of power that deserved respect.

Still, there was the matter of the sunken profits. And if this man stayed and continued these spectacular healings, He would draw the attention of the Jewish authorities to their illegal business. The Pharisees would not take kindly to the notion of Jews raising pigs. No one in his right mind wanted to incur the wrath of the powerful high priest. This stranger obviously had not given much thought to the hardship He had created for their town.

It had not escaped the mob's notice that some of the disciples were armed with swords. The freed demoniacs, also, might take fierce exception to any physical action to drive away their new Friend and Rescuer.

After serious deliberation, the townspeople instructed the boldest of their number to ask Jesus to leave, and pushed him to the front of the crowd. The unhappy spokesman, anxious to deliver his message without antagonizing the unwelcome, powerful visitor, blurted out his request.

"Please, Sir, we are simple townspeople. We mean no personal disrespect to you, but if you stay, you will bring great trouble on us. We want you to leave."

The rest of the crowd added their voices to his request. The surprised crowd watched in relief as Jesus stepped at once into the boat. His disciples followed, not neglecting to complain about the mob's discourtesy. Refusing hospitality to a visitor was a serious breach of the rigid Jewish social code, which Peter was of a mind to point out.

"You not only healed those two men, Lord. You made it safe for them all to live and work here. They can raise more pigs. This crowd should be punished for being so ungrateful."

"They have already punished themselves, Simon. No one else here can receive healing or any other help from me."

"Master, wait!" One of the healed demoniacs ran to the boat. "Take me with you, Master. Let me be one of your followers. I want to help with your work."

"No, go home and tell everyone how much God has done for you, and the mercy He has shown you."

The disciples pushed the boat away from the shore. Ariel and Tobias again took their places on each side of the vessel. Jesus immediately fell asleep. Tobias, keeping a watchful eye on his sleeping charge, concluded that Jesus' weariness had as much to do with the rejection He had just experienced as it did with His being awakened to quell the storm.

"I'll never understand these human creatures," Tobias thought out loud. "The Gadarenes eventually got accustomed to having demons in their area, but they're afraid of Prince Jesus; and all He wants to do is help them."

Son of My Love

"It's a good thing angels don't age," Ariel sighed. "I love the Prince more than my own life, but if I were mortal, the chances that young fellow takes would have already cut twenty years off my life span. I don't know what He is trying to accomplish down here, but I know Satan wants to kill Him because His Father drove Satan out of Heaven."

"Satan *will* kill Him if he sees an opportunity. We can never let our guard down for an instant. Satan probably stirred up that storm. I wish God would tell the Prince to go Home. Whatever God has in mind, surely it can't be worth risking His Son's life."

CHAPTER EIGHT

Palms of Victory

WITH PALM BRANCHES IN THEIR HANDS, people swarmed into the street, trying to catch a glimpse of the approaching procession. One man threw his cloak on the street as the donkey carrying the honored visitor came in sight. Then a woman spread her scarf over the paving stones. Excitement ran through the throng, leaping from person to person. Children broke into singing, and the crowd tossed their palm branches on the garments lying in the street.

The man riding the donkey was a descendant of the royal house of David, Israel's great warrior king. Surely this man was the one for whom they had waited so long, the leader who could free them from the suffocating grip of Roman oppression. Word of His miraculous power had been spreading through Israel for three years. Anyone who could feed over five thousand with a small lunch could also feed an army. And anyone who could raise the dead obviously had all the power of God at His command.

"Who is this?" one visitor to Jerusalem asked.

"This is Jesus, the prophet from Galilee," an elderly man answered. "The prophet Isaiah said He's the Son of the Most High God. If He can be persuaded to lead an army, we can finally be rid of the cursed Romans."

"Be careful," his wife cautioned. "Pilate brought in extra troops because of the Passover crowds, so there are more Romans around this week. One of them might hear you. You know what they did to Johannon."

The beaming disciple leading the donkey smiled at the people lining the road. At last Jesus was getting the honor He deserved. Despite questions about His birth, and being sneered at because He came from the despised village of Nazareth, He had generously poured out His time and energy to help anyone who asked for help from Him.

Unlike the disciples, Jesus' angel bodyguards were not smiling. Their greatest concern was Jesus' safety. In a huge, restless crowd like this one, any small incident could spark a riot. Somewhere in this crowd, there were surely Zealots eager to seize any chance to foment rebellion against Rome. The Romans would instantly meet any such revolt with swords and spears. At all costs, Jesus must be kept out of reach of Roman weapons.

Tobias scanned the crowd on his side of the road. "Ariel, that man in the blue cloak keeps nodding to someone on your side of the street. Keep your eye on the man near that column—the one standing in the shade."

"I've seen them both before. Anywhere the Prince goes, they are always in the crowd. They're thieves who prey on the people who follow Him, but I don't think they're dangerous. They probably don't want anything to happen to the Prince, either."

The overjoyed people, reaching past the disciples, tried to touch Jesus as He rode past.

The disciple leading the donkey turned toward the Temple. Ariel breathed a sigh of relief. As much as the Pharisees hated Jesus, they were not likely to harm Him in the Temple, especially in the midst of these cheering thousands.

Son of My Love

Perhaps, Ariel decided, *this is the Coronation God has promised His Son.* God had told Ariel, when Jesus had begun His public ministry, that Christ must die. Judging by the enormous crest of popularity the Prince was now riding, circumstances had apparently improved so much that Jesus' death would not be necessary. Jesus' enemies would be vanquished, and He would be safe. The anxiety that accompanied the heavy responsibility of protecting the Prince of Heaven would be over.

The Prince who loved the people could not be kept away from His people. To His bodyguards' chagrin, for the last three years Jesus had repeatedly put His health and even His life in jeopardy by touching people who were afflicted with contagious diseases. He had constantly moved among crowds containing violent criminals or schemers who wanted to use Him to advance their own purposes. One group had even plotted to seize Him and force Him to take the throne of David.

Jesus dismounted and gave the donkey a gentle pat. He turned it over to the care of His disciples. Tobias and Ariel stood on each side of Him, their eyes scanning the crowd. The area seemed safe. They began looking around for their fellow angels. For the Coronation of

His only Son, God would certainly want a scene of glorious splendor. There were no other angels, nothing that even hinted at a Coronation.

Jesus abruptly turned and walked into a corridor of the Temple, leaving His confused bodyguards scrambling to follow Him. Deeply disappointed, more for His sake than for their own, they dutifully kept their place beside Him. The two angels and the disciples trailed their Master as He walked through the Temple and looked around at everything. There was sorrow in Jesus' face, as if He were silently saying goodbye to something.

With the disciples and the angels following, He abandoned the Temple grounds. This route through the streets of Jerusalem took them to the road leading to Bethany. When they reached the little village two miles east of Jerusalem, Lazarus welcomed them to his home.

CHAPTER NINE

In the Place of the Dragons

JESUS AND THE DISCIPLES returned to Jerusalem the following morning. They entered the Temple grounds, and He strode directly to the court of the gentiles. He looked around at the clamor in the marketplace the Pharisees had made of the Temple, and anger covered His face like a cloud. The noise of the sacrificial animals and the haggling of the merchants and moneychangers made worship in this place impossible. The Pharisees forbade gentiles, upon pain of death, to enter the court where the Jewish men worshipped. Yet by placing this chaos in the court of the gentiles, they had, for all practical purposes, destroyed the only place of worship the gentiles had. The Pharisees would never corrupt their own court this way, but they did not hesitate to rob the gentiles of reverent contact with God.

Visitors to the Temple were also being robbed in more obvious ways. Having acceptable animals rejected as offerings, thereby being forced to needlessly buy animals from the merchants. Being cheated on the rate of exchange when they changed their foreign money into coins accepted at the Temple. Paying excessive fees for the use of ritual baths.

Jesus quietly gathered several discarded cords and began weaving them into one large rope. His disciples stood by silently, remembering the last time their Master had taken exception to the Pharisees' business practices.

"Take these things out of here! You have turned my Father's house into a den of thieves!"

Jesus reached out and jerked open the door to a cage of doves. The captive birds eagerly fled their tiny prison. Lambs ran free in the courtyard when the Carpenter untied them. Coins went dancing merrily over the stone floor. Merchants and moneychangers scurried to escape the lash.

Tobias and Ariel moved quickly among the crowd, trying to keep up with their Prince. They kept special watch on the Pharisees. Except for the Pharisees, merchants, and moneychangers, the people in the courtyard were no threat to Jesus. The Roman soldiers, at worst, appeared amused. The angels exchanged a quick, happy glance as the thieves who had invaded the gentiles' worship court fled before the lash in Jesus' hands.

This situation had been an offense to Heaven for years. The Temple had to be cleansed before the Prince would accept it and reign there. Perhaps this was why God had not allowed the Coronation yesterday. The event must be scheduled for later this week.

When the last table was overturned, Jesus stood in the center of the courtyard for a time, refusing to allow anyone to carry any vessels through the Temple enclosure.

People gathered around Jesus, and He seated Himself and began teaching them. For the rest of the day He taught and healed those who crowded around Him.

Now the Pharisees again, as they had from the beginning of His ministry, sought to discredit Him. They had chided Him this morning for accepting praise from the children. And now, using cunning religious questions, they sought to entangle Him in His speech.

Jesus instructed the people listening to Him to respect the role and teachings of the Pharisees, then set about denouncing those same religious leaders for their personal conduct and rigid traditions.

The next few days were relatively peaceful. Jesus taught in the Temple by day, returning to the Mount of Olives in the evenings to rest and talk with His disciples.

Tobias and Ariel, enjoying the respite from the hectic pace of the city, listened, unseen, along with the disciples. Jesus spoke about the coming destruction of Jerusalem and His return to Earth. His statements about His imminent death brought instant protests from the disciples. Even the two angels dismissed Jesus' talk of His Crucifixion. Over the centuries they had seen God intervene again and again to rescue His people. Joseph, Daniel, Noah, and others had been delivered from seemingly hopeless situations. God would surely do no less for His own Son.

That evening Jesus led the disciples into Jerusalem, to an upper room in a private home. The thirteen men settled themselves around a long table.

Son of My Love

Standing behind Jesus, the angels watched the meal proceed as the evening grew darker, and shadows gathered around the house. The deepening night brought back Jesus' words to Tobias and Ariel: Night is coming when no man can work.

Jesus picked up a cup. "Drink of it, all of you, for this is the new covenant in my blood, which is shed for many." He then broke the loaf of bread and gave it to them. "Take, eat; this is my body which is given for you. Do this in remembrance of me."

The conversation between the disciples turned into a squabble about who would be the greatest in the coming kingdom.

To the angels, and unnoticed by the disciples, Jesus appeared to struggle to keep back tears. While the twelve argued, He left His place at the table, removed His outer robe, and tied a towel around His waist. He poured water into a basin and knelt at the feet of one of the quarreling disciples.

The startled man, suddenly speechless, watched as Jesus washed his feet, then moved around the table, performing the same servant's chore for each of them. When He came to Peter, the blustery, impulsive fisherman found his voice. He began to argue again, but this time not about who was the greatest. Embarrassed by the fact that he, along with the other eleven, had waited, hoping one of the others would volunteer for the menial task, Peter vigorously objected.

"You shall never wash my feet, Lord!"

"Then you have no part with me."

Peter relented. When Jesus finished the duty He had given Himself, He put on His robe and returned to His place.

"You call me Master and Lord, and so I am. What I have done for you, do for each other."

He resumed His meal. "Not all of you are clean," Jesus said to the twelve. "One of you will betray me. The hand of the betrayer is on the table with me."

Amid shocked questions from the disciples, Peter quietly prompted John to ask Jesus to identify the betrayer. Jesus identified Judas to John and Peter as the one who dipped his hand in the bowl with Him.

"What you have to do, do quickly," He said to Judas.

Tobias moved as if to block Judas' path, but Jesus held out His hand to stop the angel. The nine disciples who were unaware of Judas' intentions assumed that Jesus had sent him on an errand.

Son of My Love

The sorrow writ so large on the disciples' faces moved Jesus to set aside His own grief for a moment to comfort them. He commended them for their past faithfulness. Then He spoke to them of serving God and other people, of loving one another, and of His coming suffering and triumph. He gave them His promise of a Comforter and prayed for them. A long, loving prayer filled with concern for them.

To His disciples, listening to Jesus speak to His Father about His longing to go Home, and of God's ages-long love for Him, was like being allowed to listen in on a very private, tender conversation. Almost as if they had been granted permission to eavesdrop. To the angels, hearing Christ promise peace of heart to these grieving, quarrelsome men, and entreat His Father for them when His own heart was breaking, was Jesus' greatest miracle. These eleven Galileans were so caught up in their own feelings that it had yet to occur to them to offer support and comfort to Him.

They sang a hymn and left the upper room to follow the streets that led outside the city wall. Once outside the gate they traced the familiar path to the Mount of Olives.

As they walked, Jesus said to them, "You will all desert me this night, for it is written, 'I will strike the Shepherd and the sheep will scatter.' But after I am raised to life again, I will go ahead of you to Galilee."

"Lord," Peter protested, "I will never desert you, even if everyone else does."

"Peter, before the cock will crow twice today, you will deny me three times."

The other disciples echoed Peter's protest, pledging their loyalty to Him.

When they reached Gethsemane, Jesus left eight of the disciples at the entrance. "Sit down here while I pray."

He took Peter, James, and John with Him farther into the garden. The grief and terror He had kept at bay by sheer force of His will during supper now returned, stalking Him through the dark shadows of Gethsemane.

"My soul is so heavy with sorrow that I am nearly crushed to death. Stay here. Keep awake and watch with me."

With His angels at either side, He walked deeper into the garden. Gethsemane had been a welcome haven from the endless carping of the Pharisees. Now this serene retreat had become a trap of His own choosing.

Son of My Love

At the end of the path He met Someone He had not seen face to face for thirty-three years. His Father gently dismissed the angels. "Leave us and go Home now. My Son and I need to talk privately."

With an anxious glance at their troubled Prince, the angels left Gethsemane. Jesus watched as their wings carried yet more friends away from Him. The rush of their wings faded into the night, and the deadly silence came back.

"Thank you, Father, for coming down here. I know you always hear me when I pray, but it is good to have you here in the garden."

"I came because my Son needs me near Him now. In a few hours I will have to leave Him Fatherless." The Father extended His hand to take His Son's trembling hand. "I know that the pain, as terrible as it will be, is only part of the agony you face. Is that not true, Son?"

"Yes." The word was a dry whisper. "Just when I think there could be no new horrors left, another one lunges at me with its fangs bared. Now I understand why that psalm speaks of being surrounded by a pack of wild dogs."

"Then come and let us talk while we can."

While His Father held Him, Jesus gripped God's hand tightly, letting His terror and heartbreak tumble forth in faltering words that made the darkness seem suffocating. When there were no words left, He knelt at His Father's feet.

CHAPTER TEN

Gethsemane

THE MOON STANDS STILL, the night birds call, the shadows play across the land.

The Son of God kneels to pray, His fate resting in His Father's hand.

Cold shadows, cold moon, cold world. Where are those who have called Him their Lord?

The Abyss awaits. Death, in Roman sandals, mocks His Father's word.

"You are my beloved Son. Upon you, Child, have I set my love.

The Prince of Life for sinful man, his Hope, his Door to life above."

"Father, all things are in your hand, all things possible unto you.

Your will, not mine, be done. Whatever you ask of me, I will do."

"I will not say, Son, there is no pain, no shame, on that dreadful road;

For Calvary is there, with crown of thorns, Roman spear, scourge, and goad."

"Abba, must I drink this bitter cup? Is there not another way?

The cup is filled with sin, which never touched me. My soul shrinks away."

"There is no other way, Son. For man's redemption blood must be shed.

There's no other worthy. No angel or man can act in your stead.

Would that I could take your place, for I would give my own life for you.

But I can't stand in your lonely place. I can't pay the debt come due.

All those millions of years I loved you, my only begotten Son.

We worked together, you and I, to build Earth's frame and light the sun.

You shared my work of creation; you were part of my every plan.

Son of My Love

There was no jealousy in you when I chose to create the man.

Now you are all that stands between man and a destiny in Hell.

Your life on Earth has shown man my grace--a life that Judas will sell."

Twice Jesus rises to seek comfort from the friends who wait for Him.

Twice they have slept. "Could you not watch just one hour?" He asks of them.

He returns to His Father and kneels. Blood drops seep onto His brow.

He falls to His face, and all Creation hangs in the balance now.

Tears and blood mingle with dirt. "Abba, will you be there on that hill?

Or will I be alone? Don't leave me, like friends and disciples will."

"I'll walk with you on the road, Son, but I must leave you at the cross.

I can't look at sin, and you must become sin, to save man from loss.

The separation you dread will come. Through pain you will cry for me.

I cannot answer then, and my own grief will match
your agony."
God helps His Son to His feet, and Jesus clings to His
Father's hand.
"If you can't face this fiery trial, my Child, I will
understand.
I will love you no less, could love you no less; you're
the heart of me.
My army waits. Ask of me at any time. I will set you
free.
I will not force Calvary on you, will not make you face
the grave.
You will be free to come Home with me, but man will
stay Satan's slave.
There will never be another chance. I can't save both
man and you.
Our time grows short; the Temple soldiers march.
My Son, what will you do?"
"If there be no other way, Lord, not my will but your
own be done."
The Father caresses His Son's blood-covered brow.
"I know, my Son,
You left Heaven for me, as well as for the fallen
human race.

Son of My Love

You knew how much I cared for man. You read the
heartache in my face.

You and I must go now, Son, back to the place your
disciples wait.

There's so much I want to tell you, and Judas is
nearing the gate."

Father and Son walk side by side along the path to
destiny.

"My Son, one day this whole world will know how
much my Prince means to me.

But before the crown must come the cross. The earth
will shake in her strife,

The sky turn black as I walk away from you, the Light
of my life."

God takes His Son in His mighty arms. "When all
you can do is trust,

Son, as you yield your final breath, believe I love you,
and I'm just.

Nothing can separate us for long; not the soldiers,
who are here.

They can't see me, but we know, my Son, now and
always I am near.

Joy will come in that bright morning when you walk
away from the grave,

And Earth will rejoice to welcome back my fair
Prince, who died to save."

CHAPTER ELEVEN

Calvary

THE WHIP, TIPPED WITH SHARP bits of bone and metal, cut again and again into the prisoner's back. Roman lictors lunged forward to apply maximum force. Barbed leather lashes tore out bits of flesh and left raw, bleeding stripes. Lash after lash, stripe upon stripe, over the bruises left by the beating from the high priest's soldiers the night before. His head jerked backward in a reflex as each blow fell.

From above, an anguished Father, who had just left Earth and His Son's side, watched the torture of His only Son. The young Prince bore the abuse in silence, refusing to cry out for mercy from His tormentors, or for rescue by His Father.

Billions of other eyes looked down on the grim scene. God's angel army watched, waiting for the order to strike and snatch their beloved Commander away from His enemies.

The Roman soldiers untied Jesus' wrists. Shivering from shock and loss of blood, He stumbled back from the post. One soldier, amused by Jesus' claims of kingship, had been weaving a thorny branch into a circle. He pressed the mock crown down on Jesus' head, and two-inch-long thorns cut like nails into His scalp, sending blood streaming into His eyes.

In the front rank of countless angels, in the very center of the group, an angry Michael stood beside the Father. The second-ranking commander of God's army turned sharply to face his soldiers. "I'm going to stop this! The Prince has never harmed anyone. He doesn't deserve this punishment."

"No, Michael." God's voice was heavy with pain. "My Son must see this through to the end. This day will test everyone. I want your word that you won't intervene, unless Jesus asks to be released."

"Your Majesty, this is not right."

"I will make it right, in my own time. Your word, Michael?"

Son of My Love

Michael stared down at the young man being battered by Pilate's soldiers. The archangel turned to the Father, his eyes silently pleading with God.

"Michael?" God asked again.

"You have my word, Lord. I will do nothing against your orders."

"You do not have to stay here and watch this, Michael. Leave if you wish."

"I would not feel right about turning my back and walking away from Him. Watching is the only way I have of standing by Him, and you. You have to be suffering more than any of the rest of us. He is our Friend, but He is your Son."

"You do not want to walk away, nor do I, but I will have no choice. You must understand that Tobias and Ariel cannot leave here under any circumstances."

"Yes, Lord. It will be done, as you say."

A soldier roughly placed a crossbeam on Jesus' bleeding back. The heavy beam dug splinters into the stripes on His shoulders. Christ fell, and a soldier dragged a bystander to Jesus' side to shoulder the crossbeam.

At the end of the brutal climb, the soldiers stretched out His arms and nailed His wrists to the wood. They lifted the crossbeam and fastened it to the upright beam.

Tobias felt his hands grasping the edge of the parapet. His anger clamped his hands in a fierce grip around the top of the wall. After all the Prince had done to relieve human suffering, the ungrateful creatures were repaying Him with nails and thorns. Tobias' rage was boiling up inside him, pushing aside his grief. Undoubtedly the order to strike would come soon. God could not endure watching this horror much longer.

Jesus' less impulsive bodyguard was going through the same internal war. Ariel was standing as if frozen in place, but one hand was wrapped tightly around the hilt of his sword.

Michael caught sight of someone in the mob, just beyond the line of soldiers holding back the spectators. While others in the crowd were either screaming insults at Christ or weeping, the old man who had caught Michael's attention was celebrating. Michael gazed intently at him. Recognition suddenly flared. He was not an old man. He was an old enemy, Satan! Beside Satan stood Moloch, one of the demons which had always wholeheartedly followed Satan's lead. Satan's glee over Christ's suffering almost caused Michael's promise to God to dissolve in blazing fury. Michael took a tighter hold on his emotions. *God should have let me do away with Satan when I defeated him in that war, or when I stopped him from stealing Moses' body. Now the Prince is the one paying because Satan was allowed to live.*

God had felt the tearing pain as the spikes had pierced Jesus' flesh. Now He was feeling the piercing of His Son's spirit as a crushing load of guilt for wrongs the Son had never committed pressed down on Jesus.

Taunting calls from people passing by the cross added to the burden building up on the Son's sturdy shoulders. Michael could see in the Father's face the natural longing of a good parent to rush to the aid of a suffering child.

Three hours crawled by, and the taunts increased. The only way Jesus could breathe was to push Himself up on the merciless spikes. God heard His Son speak, securing a haven for His mother. Jesus pleaded for mercy for the men who were killing Him, and granted life to the repentant thief.

God turned His face from His Son and walked away. Darkness blotted out the sun. Three more hours dragged themselves across the horizon. God stood resolutely, refusing to look at His Son.

Jesus' scream of agony and abandonment reached across the great gulf between Heaven and Earth, tearing at God's heart. From his position near the parapet, Ariel saw God flinch and cover His face at the sound of that desperate cry.

Tobias and Ariel had not heard God's order to Michael to not intervene. God had told Ariel three years ago that Jesus must die, but surely the Father would not stand by that statement now, not in the face of the brutality being inflicted on His only Son. Considering a course of action was one thing, but actually standing by and doing nothing as scheming Pharisees and barbaric Romans savaged Jesus was another matter entirely. This could not be what God wanted. The just God who had allowed a guilty Satan to live after his rebellion could not allow His innocent, obedient Son to die. Yet the Prince was going to die, in a very few minutes, if someone did not remove Him from that cross.

Confused by God's mysterious failure to act, Ariel had taken his hand from his sword. Now his hand reached again, uncertainly, for the weapon, and Tobias followed his lead. God nodded to Michael. Powerful hands clamped down on Ariel's and Tobias' arms.

God whispered to His Son's spirit, "It is enough of the Crucifixion, my Son."

On Calvary, Jesus accepted the drink He had earlier refused so that His parched throat could speak His last message. "It is finished! Father, my spirit is in your hands." His head fell forward, and death closed His eyes.

A great rumbling began as the earth writhed. The giant curtain that separated the Temple's Holy of Holies from the people was ripped apart from top to bottom, as if torn by an invisible hand.

Michael saw the cross sway in the earthquake. At least now the Prince was not feeling the tearing nails as the cross rocked in the turmoil.

Michael's sympathetic spirit was outraged by Satan's gloating remarks to Moloch as the two outcasts lingered near the cross.

"I knew that if I caused the worthless humans enough misery, God would do something foolish to try to rescue them. But I never, in my wildest imaginings, seriously believed He would put that pampered Son of His at risk. I thought God would allow Him to teach and preach for a while, then take Him Home to safety."

Sensing Michael's eyes on him, Satan looked up at his old nemesis and smiled mockingly. After all these centuries, the humiliating memory of Michael's ruinous rout of Satan's criminal army still stung. It had been a titanic blow to Satan's pride.

To Satan's mind, Michael and Gabriel had been fools not to join the rebellion, and Satan had told them so at the time. The combined power of the three mightiest creatures God had ever created could have given them the universe. Now all the loyal archangels had left was the bloody corpse of the Prince they had served so faithfully.

Michael saw Satan and Moloch turn to leave. In the cauldron of Michael's emotions, one fact rose to the surface. Satan would never have been able to defeat God militarily or harm Him physically. So he had taken the coward's option of striking like the snake he was at the center of God's life, His Son, while the Son was vulnerable in the robe of human flesh. It was indeed, as Jesus had cried out, finished. And Satan had won.

Joseph of Arimathea left to seek Pilate's permission to claim Jesus' body. He returned shortly with instructions from Pilate for the soldiers to release the body to him.

God was standing at the parapet, staring down at the faithful few who were struggling to care for Jesus' body. The beginning of the sabbath was too near for Jesus to be given the complete, traditional burial ritual.

Michael walked to the Father's side, intending to offer whatever was left of comfort or consolation. "The Prince's actions were the greatest display of courage I have ever seen, Lord. As agonizing as this day was for you, you must be unspeakably proud of Him."

"Yes, I am. Sometimes Satan would accidentally tell the truth. Just before he was driven out of here, he said I thought the sun rose and set on my Son." He looked on as John, Joseph, Nicodemus, and a few of Jesus' other followers rolled an enormous stone across the door of the tomb. "Today is His sunset."

CHAPTER TWELVE

John 17:24

THE FATHER TURNS HIS anguished face away
From a blood-red sunset at Calv'ry's rim.
Red as the blood that His Son shed this day.
He weeps for His Son, but who weeps for Him?
As God speaks, tears of blood stream from His eyes.
Tears of compassion, grief, great love, and pride.
"Were the souls of men really worth this Price?
Thirty-three years He was gone from my side.
Before suns or stars or time came to be
He graced Heaven's courts, this strong Son of mine.
Earth needed sun and moon so man could see,
But Christ was the Light that made Heaven shine.
Man says that love grows greater through the years.
My love for Christ grew through eternity.

Son of My Love

I said goodbye, watched Him leave through my
tears—
Leave for war. Through tears, I could hardly see.
It was my plan, but it was His great heart
That made that plan real. He wanted to go.
Herod's murderous rage was just the start.
Danger worse than Herod waited below.
His cross stands empty on Golgotha's hill,
My Son and my Joy, and my Soldier brave.
In Gethsemane He bowed to my will.
I gave you my Best; you gave Him a grave.
'Why did You forsake me?' I heard Him call.
I heard, but I had no comfort to give.
Man's sin, not His, placed between us that wall.
My Child must die so that mankind might live."
Two long nights pass after they take Him down.
One dawn gone now, another on the way.
"I must get out my Son's victory crown.
I saved it for Him, kept it for this day.
See that golden glow at the garden tomb?
It isn't sunrise through the olive trees.
It's the Light of hope, and it's Satan's doom.
My Soldier arrives—the enemy flees.
He's not the same; He has scars on His brow.

We both have scars. Mine are hidden inside.
They will always be there, but they're soothed now
By joy of a Father's pride justified.
No medals or ribbons for this campaign,
Though He has triumphed over death and sin.
But His gallant battle was not waged in vain.
I will award Him the saved souls of men.
Forty more days, then my Son will come home.
Forty days seem like a thousand or more.
Michael and Gabriel, they wait by His throne.
I will watch for Him, wait by Heaven's door."

CHAPTER THIRTEEN

The Ransom

THE METAL SHACKLES HOLDING the prisoner's punctured wrists to the cavern wall were blast-furnace hot, adding more agony to the searing pain in the torn wrists. Relentless pain pulsed unmercifully through the battered face, no longer recognizable as human. The rough cavern wall ground dirt into the captive's ripped back, where ribs showed through the deepest wounds.

Just beyond the cavern walls, the earth's molten core roiled with heat so intense that rocks melted, and metal deposits in the rocks liquefied. Scalding steam and sulfuric fumes seeped through fissures in the earth. The noxious mist swirling through the caverns burned the prisoner's lungs. From somewhere in the darkness He could hear screams and moans. The only light was a dim glow from fire burning in a deep pit in the caverns.

Through a fog of pain and blood the captive could see a massive shape moving through the darkness. The shape became clearer as it moved closer to Him. It stopped in front of Him, and through eyes swollen almost shut the man stared at His tormentor. Tall and imposing, the creature carried himself with the arrogance of a bully no one dares challenge. His once beautiful features were overlaid with cruelty. Contempt for his royal prisoner added another layer of ugliness to his face.

"How much longer do you think you can hold out, Your Highness?" His use of the term of respect was a taunt. "The pain isn't going to lessen. All you have to do is switch allegiances, and you can go free."

"No." The man's swollen lips made speaking torture. "You made me that same offer three years ago. My answer was no. It's still no. Your price for bread was too high in the wilderness, and your price for water is too high here."

"Thirst will bring you to it. That's the one thing that brings everyone down here around eventually." He held out a cup of water. "Your throat must be burning like those shackles." He moved the cup closer to the man's mouth. "Go on. Take it."

The Prince shook His head, and the infuriated creature dashed the water into the man's face. Struggling against waves of pain, the captive turned His head to brush His face against His shoulder, wiping away the water, making sure He did not swallow any of it. His act of rejection sent the creature into a screaming tirade.

"Yes, you are your Father's Son--stubborn to the point of death. It's too bad He can't share your fate." He flung the cup away, and it bounced off the far wall. "That was your last chance. The next time I offer you a drink, you will beg me for it." He leaned against the opposite wall and folded his arms across his chest. "Having you under my control should be satisfaction enough, but it isn't. I want to see God's spoiled Son kneeling at my feet, and before this is over, I will. Most of all, I'm looking forward to seeing the look on God's face when that happens. All I heard out of your Father when I lived in Heaven was 'my Son this...' and 'my Son that...' I had your name crammed down my throat until I was sick of hearing it. Everything He did, everything He made, was for you. And He drove me out of Heaven because He saw me as a threat to you." He aimed another insult over his shoulder as he turned to leave. "He was right. I would have killed you up there, but He had you so well protected I couldn't get to you."

A light shock rumbled through the caverns. The creature turned his eyes toward the ceiling and smiled as a thin dusting of dirt drifted down. "A little leftover shock from the great Friday earthquake. Your Father is still grieving over you. But that will stop, in time. When He finally admits to Himself that you're never coming Home again, He will find someone else to shower His affection on. He has to have someone to love. That's His nature." He began walking away. "I will be back in a few hours. I'll give you some time to think about your disrespectful attitude toward me. We will see how defiant you still are after a few more hours of my hospitality. Although I must admit that you've endured this place remarkably well. These last two days would have broken anyone else."

"That 'little leftover shock' was more than grief, Lucifer," Jesus called after him. "It was a warning. You have something that belongs to God, and He wants it back."

Lucifer stopped and jerked around angrily. "His Son, I suppose?" he sneered.

"Yes, His Son." Moving His parched lips to speak was agonizing, but maintaining His defiance of Satan was vital. "Nothing you have done to me can change the fact that my Father loves me."

"Oh, I'm sure He wants you back, Lord Prince. He would take Hell apart--and me with it--if that would bring you Home to Him. But He can't allow you back in Heaven. You're tainted now with all that sin that was placed on you."

"I didn't swallow any of that poison, and I'm not swallowing your lies."

"You and I both saw your Father turn His back on you. I don't understand your refusing to give in. You don't have to fear His wrath. You're already in Hell. What more can He do to you?" He shrugged. "I have all the time in the world. You will come around."

Jesus watched Satan disappear into the shadows. Pushing against the shackles on His wrists and ankles, He moved Himself a fraction of an inch away from the wall, giving His slashed back a tiny moment of relief; but doubling the pain in His limbs. When He could no longer bear the agony of His weight against the shackles, He sank back against the wall, feeling the roughness again grinding against His lacerated back.

Two days and a night of moving from pain to pain had ground the suffering into His spirit as well as His body. But His granite determination to keep His soul beyond Satan's reach had helped keep Him from sinking beneath the blackness inching toward Him like dark waters.

There was no sun here, no movement of light and shadow to mark off the hours, but He knew there were at least twelve hours left before dawn. He had to survive those twelve endless hours. He had publicly staked His ability to verify His message on His power to leave this place.

He pushed Himself forward again, trying to relieve the pressure on His back. The familiar bolts of pain His movements sent through His wrists and ankles reminded Him that the relief for His back would be short lived.

Hour after creeping hour He repeated those movements. Hot shackles and cutting rocks and sulfuric mist vied with each other in inflicting suffering.

Four thousand miles above, in a grave carved into stone, two pinpoints of light began to grow. As they expanded, they pushed back the darkness until the only shadows left in the crypt were puddles of blackness in the corners. The glowing lights stretched taller; and the figures inhabiting the lights became more and more well defined until two angels, wings folded, stood side by side. Ariel was holding a handsome pair of leather sandals, and Tobias carried a pure white linen robe.

The physical coldness of the rock tomb paled beside the coldness of spirit the angels felt as they stared at the lifeless shape outlined by the graveclothes wrapped around it. Ariel and Tobias had been charged with protecting Him since before His birth. They had guarded the lively toddler, who had chased butterflies and scorpions with equal enthusiasm. Through His growing-up years they had kept danger away from Him, and cared for the hungry, exhausted young man after His bout with Satan in the wilderness. God's occasional word of approval for their efforts on His Son's behalf had been rewarding; but their motive, always, had been pure, simple love for this Prince of Heaven.

Ariel wearily shook his head. He and Tobias sank down on a rock shelf and stared at the still form on the stone slab. Even though he and Tobias had been following God's instructions when they had stepped back and allowed the Crucifixion to take its course, they still felt an overwhelming sense of failure. That thirty-three years of constant vigilance should come to this--an unwashed, hastily buried body wrapped in bloody graveclothes.

Tobias, knowing the great stone over the door would keep the squad of sixteen Roman soldiers outside from hearing him, began questioning Ariel about their orders.

"What did His Father say we're supposed to do with the Prince's robe and sandals? Are we to dress His body in them?"

"All God told me was that we were to bring them here and wait."

"Wait for what? And for how long?"

"That was all He said. Just to stay inside the tomb and wait."

Tobias smoothed the folded robe. "It seems a shame to just leave His body there in that bloody sheet. He deserves better than that."

"I know, but we can't go against God's instructions."

"God must be so grief stricken that He isn't thinking straight. He loved His Son so much that His whole world revolved around that young man. He can't accept the fact that the Prince is dead. And He is probably blaming Himself, because He sent the Prince down here."

"I suppose not even God is immune to grief. I don't like leaving His body uncared for either, Tobias, but we have to obey orders. Even if they don't make sense to us."

They settled back against the stone wall and prepared to wait for whatever action God was planning to take. *It could be,* Tobias mused, *that the splendid robe and sandals were for a full-scale royal funeral. Perhaps the Father was planning such a funeral for the Prince. It could also be that, after the funeral, He would unleash His army to avenge the brutal murder of His only Son.*

Ariel was wrapped in misery the way the Prince's forlorn, unattended body was wrapped in graveclothes. The last time Ariel had seen God face to face, until this week, had been three years ago, at the beginning of Jesus' public ministry. Alarmed at the seething hostility among the jealous Pharisees, Ariel had left Jesus under Tobias' protection and returned to Heaven to plead with the Father.

God looked down at the angel standing at the foot of the throne. "Ariel, you're supposed to be guarding my Son. Did you desert your post?"

"No, Your Majesty. Tobias is with Him. I came back here because I'm concerned about the Prince. Those evil men hate Him, Lord. If He keeps clashing with them, they're going to kill Him."

"And what do you wish me to do, Ariel?"

"Please, Lord, tell Him to come Home. He won't listen to anyone but you."

"I can't do that, Ariel. He has to stay down there. And yes, eventually, they are going to kill Him. When He is arrested, you must not interfere under any circumstances."

God's seeming callousness sent a jolt of shocked disbelief through Ariel's soul. "Lord, He is your *Son!*"

"He is my universe, Ariel. Everything I ever loved is wrapped up in that young man. I know you and Tobias and the other angels love Him, but I love Him more than you can ever begin to understand, and I still can't bring Him Home. I'm sorry you are hurt. I never wanted anyone to suffer, but His death has to be."

Ariel's mind returned to the present, to the tomb and the unending wait. After a few minutes, his thoughts wandered again, this time to Jesus' arrest three nights ago.

He and Tobias had been sent Home just before Jesus had been arrested. They and the rest of Heaven had stood horrified, looking over the parapet of Home as the

Pharisees had broken their own laws to hand one of their own people over to the hated Roman overlords.

Michael, Jesus' second in command, watched the Father's face as Jesus underwent the kind of flogging that tore flesh from bone. Torn between loyalty to God and compassion for the suffering Prince, Michael held back on giving the order he so desperately wanted to give.

Leaving Michael with final instructions to keep the army in check, and allow no intervention unless Jesus asked to be rescued, God walked away from His Son, and the sky turned black. Ariel saw God flinch in agony when He heard His Son cry out to Him. In an obviously prearranged signal, God had nodded to Michael, and Ariel and Tobias had found themselves being removed elsewhere by archangels Gabriel and Raphael.

Ariel sighed as he looked down at the pair of beautiful sandals he was holding. Revolt against the Father would have been futile, even if he had been inclined to rebellion. The entire angelic army could not have stood against God.

Though God had always maintained that He was not compelled to explain any of His actions to anyone, He had been gracious enough to offer two words to the army His Son had always commanded. "Trust me," the Father had said to them. "Trust me," as His Son's body was laid in the tomb, and the Prince's soul had vanished into Satan's kingdom.

CHAPTER FOURTEEN

Resurrection

JESUS SHIFTED HIS WRISTS around in the shackles the best way He could, to move the nail wounds away from the hot metal digging at those wounds. Less than three hours until sunrise. To keep His mind off this place and the suffering slashing Him, He concentrated on thinking about Home. Green fields and parks and fountains. Gleaming palaces, with their gardens and courtyards overflowing with flowers. Countless angels, and light and music everywhere. Most of all, His Father's face.

Twice in the last three years, God had spoken from Home, publicly proclaiming His pride in His Son. That Fatherly pride was not going to be sullied by any action of His, Jesus had determined. He was going to return to God the way He had left. Satan was never going to be able to fling any taunts about His behavior into His Father's face.

Moloch, one of Satan's lieutenants, drifted in and out of the chamber from time to time, checking on the prisoner and reporting to his master. Moloch looked nothing like the idols of him fashioned by the ancient Canaanites. He resembled a cross between a scorpion and a poison toad, with a moral character to match. His hatred of Jesus nearly matched Satan's, and he was obviously enjoying watching Jesus struggle in the shackles.

Moloch had entertained himself at will on Earth, toying with and tormenting people--until Jesus had appeared on the scene three years ago. The young intruder from Nazareth had made life miserable for Moloch and his cohorts, driving them out of their human victims, constantly forcing Moloch and the others from place to place. They had eagerly watched for a chance to rid themselves of Him, until they had found willing tools in Caiaphas and Judas.

Less than an hour to endure now. Moloch returned, followed shortly by his master.

Satan, trying to decide how close Jesus was to giving in, watched the captive for a few minutes. "Are you ready to listen to reason now, Your Highness?"

Jesus shook His head. "I won't help you hurt my Father."

"He obviously doesn't care how much you hurt." Satan affected an air of amused patience. "You don't owe Him anything. He has abandoned you in favor of the human race. How does it feel to come in second, Lord?" When Jesus did not answer, Satan continued his verbal attack. "He told you to trust Him, didn't He? And you don't want to admit that you were deceived by your own Father."

"If something has gone wrong, and He has been forced to abandon me down here, He is still better than you. He was motivated by wanting to help people. You never cared about anyone but yourself."

Satan settled into his favorite comfortable pose, leaning against the opposite wall, his arms across his chest. "Such loyalty," he said sarcastically. "I suppose a Prince must behave like a Prince, even in Hell. I don't subscribe to such outdated notions myself."

"Don't concern yourself, Lucifer. No one who really knows you will ever mistake you for a gentleman."

Satan hesitated, then decided to ignore that remark in order to pursue his objective of persuading Jesus to join him. "Why don't we both just forget about the incident with the water cup yesterday? Since you can never leave here, you might as well join me. It isn't such a bad life, once you get used to it. At least, down here, I'm free. I'm not under God's domination."

"For someone who says he values freedom, you don't mind enslaving others."

"You're intelligent enough to be of great service to me. Just on a human level, even discounting your divinity, you're a very astute young man. You can be of help to me, and I can make life a lot less painful for you."

Jesus leaned back against the wall to give His wrists and feet a rest. "No."

"Come now, Lord Prince. How long are you going to continue this painful foolishness?"

"As long as necessary, Lucifer." He lifted up a silent plea. *Please, Father, help me endure these few remaining minutes.*

Lucifer walked closer. "We're really not that different, Prince Jesus. After all, in Heaven we were both brilliant and powerful and handsome. I can't understand why your Father gave you such an ordinary-looking appearance on Earth. Probably some notion about wanting you to appear more human. And you haven't fared very well these last few days, either. It seems I have ended up being the better-looking of the two. What a difference a few days can make. This time last week you were the national hero."

Just a few more minutes, Jesus reminded Himself as He moved His scarred back away from the wall.

Lucifer walked another step closer. "I would give a lot to know what you're thinking right now, but I can't read the thoughts of others like you can. That's another gift your Father gave you that He gave no one else." Satan's smile was half menace, half persuasion. "And I really would like to know what you and He talked about in the garden just before your arrest. I assume you dreaded the prospect of becoming my captive."

"My conversation with my Father is none of your business. Assume what you will."

Lucifer dismissed Jesus' defiance. "Brave talk from a prisoner. But then, you are a brave man. Even I will concede that."

"And you are a coward, Satan. You waited until you knew I was weak and starved before you appeared in the wilderness. And you didn't start that war in Heaven because you were brave. You thought Michael would join you and bring the army with him. You intended to hide behind them."

"It would have been foolish of me to challenge you at the peak of your strength. Courage is an overrated trait, Lord. You're right, of course. When I approached Michael with my proposal that we join forces, he went straight to your Father."

"That is called loyalty, Lucifer." The hot metal was digging deeper into the nail wounds. The pain throbbing in His bruised face seemed to claw past skin and muscles, reaching for His soul. He turned His head to look at His enemy, His gaze boring into Satan's eyes. "You wish to know what I'm thinking? I will tell you. Killing me won't bring you my inheritance, as you hoped it would. My Father isn't going to walk away and abandon to you everything He created for me, no matter how grief-stricken He is."

A low animal snarl tore its way out of Satan's throat. "I'm done with cajoling and reasoning with you, my fine Prince. Your Father always tried to make the universe revolve around you--even promising you His whole kingdom, and giving you command of the army. Not because you had earned it, but because you were His

Son." Satan's ages-old hatred blazed from eyes burning
with malice. "What is worse, He made Michael your
second in command. Michael! As if I could not be
trusted."

Jesus, lungs burning from fumes, gasped for breath.
"It was His kingdom to give, Satan, and you could never
be trusted." By sheer force of His will, He moved
Himself away from the wall, pushing Himself up to His
full height. "Just before I died, my Father gave me a
message for you."

"No!" Satan shrieked. He slammed Jesus' head back
against the wall, seizing Jesus' throat in a vise grip with
one hand, digging the fingers of his other hand into the
wounds in His face. His clawing attack sent fiery waves
of anguish through Jesus' body. "I don't want to hear
anything from you. If your Father has anything to say to
me, He can tell me Himself." He slammed Jesus' head
against the wall again, with all the force he could gather.
He was screaming now. All pretense of control was
gone. "Do you hear me? I want to hear it from God
Himself."

"Lucifer!" thundered a voice from above them, "take
your filthy, murdering hands off my Son!"

The force of the voice roaring that command, like an enraged lion through the canyons of Hell, shook the ground, knocking Satan and Moloch off their feet. Moloch scrambled wildly to put what he hoped was lightning-bolt distance between himself and Satan. Not sure where the voice was coming from, he pressed back against the wall, trying to hide in a convenient shadow. Maybe the fact that he had not actively participated in the torture would save his life.

Satan climbed to his feet, looking around warily to see if the Source of that voice had actually invaded his kingdom. He did not see the Father, but the voice came again.

"Move away from Him, Lucifer. Don't touch Him again."

Satan backed away. He had always calculated how far he could push God, backing down before he crossed the line into destruction. Now he was in uncharted territory. He had tortured and murdered the Light of God's life, disrupting the Father-Son relationship with which no one had ever been allowed to interfere.

Jesus laughed at Satan's stunned expression. "Ask and you shall receive, Lucifer. You wanted to hear from my Father, and He has accommodated you."

Lucifer watched in cold fury as the shackles fell from Jesus' wrists and ankles. Blood and dirt disappeared from His body. The raw wounds closed, leaving scars only in His wrists and side.

God's voice spoke again, tenderly this time. "I am so deeply proud of you, Son. We must leave the scars in your wrists and side, for now. You will need them to identify yourself. We can remove them later, if you wish."

Jesus turned His full attention to Lucifer. "What a difference a few minutes can make, Lucifer. A few minutes ago, you were done with cajoling and reasoning with me."

Jesus stepped away from the wall, and Satan moved backward. Moloch was standing against the opposite wall, so still that he could have been carved from stone. He had not the slightest intention of being caught between the Prince and his own master, regardless of whatever satanic wrath he would face later because of his caution. If God wanted His only Son back, that was God's business. Besides, Jesus, free of the shackles, healed, and returned to full strength, looked much too able to take care of Himself for Moloch's comfort.

"Take his keys, Son," the voice from above called.

Jesus reached out His hand. "I'll take your keys, Lucifer."

Lucifer's rage briefly overwhelmed his better judgment. "No, you won't. This is my kingdom. You don't rule here."

Mad with hatred, Lucifer swung his arm and aimed a blow at Jesus' head. He was hurled instantly against the wall when his arm connected with a white-hot wall of light that suddenly flashed between him and Jesus.

"Lucifer, that was your last warning," the Father's angry voice roared. "If you value your existence, don't ever touch my Child again."

"You are wrong, Satan," Jesus answered. "My Father and I rule everywhere, including here." He reached out His hand. "My Abba wants your keys, and I intend to see that He gets them." When Satan hesitated, Jesus prodded his memory. "You said it yourself, Satan. He would take Hell apart and you with it to get His Son back, and His Son isn't leaving without the keys."

Satan cautiously extended the hand holding the keys.

Jesus smiled. "Careful, Lucifer. My Father told you not to touch me."

Satan's hand stopped in mid-reach. "Moloch, come here. Give the Prince the keys."

Moloch, unhappy about having divine attention focused on him, eyed the keys as if they were made of molten lava.

"His Father didn't tell *you* not to touch Him," Satan snapped desperately. "Give His Highness the keys." This time, Satan's use of the royal title contained no trace of his earlier taunts.

Reasoning that the sooner Jesus took possession of the keys, the sooner He would leave, Moloch overcame enough of his terror to obey his master. He sidled over to Satan's side, took the keys from him, and gingerly dropped them into Jesus' hand, taking infinite care not to touch the former captive.

Jesus gripped the keys firmly. "I have a brief preaching tour planned before I return to the surface, Lucifer. If you have any good judgment left at all, you won't even try to interfere."

"As I told you before, Lord Prince, I'm not foolish enough to challenge you at the peak of your strength. My temporary lapse in judgment won't be repeated. I have no illusions about what God will do to me if I try to harm His Son again."

God's voice broke the silence. "I will meet you at the door of Home forty days from now, Son. It has been so many years since you have been Home. I am looking forward to having you back beside me. If there is anything you want during these next forty days--or at any other time--you know that all you have to do is ask."

Jesus vanished in a dazzling burst of light, leaving Satan and Moloch to deal with each other.

CHAPTER FIFTEEN

Morning Light

TOBIAS MOVED RESTLESSLY, the rustle of his wings disturbing the desolate silence in the tomb. "Ariel, it's almost dawn. Maybe you misunderstood God. Ask Him about our orders. He won't get angry with you for just trying to understand His instructions."

"I heard Him clearly, Tobias. We have to wait, no matter how long it takes."

Tobias closed his eyes to shut out, if only for a few minutes, the sight of the lifeless body of his Friend. He opened his eyes just as a brilliant surge of light, so bright that it drove every shadow from the tomb and turned the inside of the crypt noonday bright, enveloped the

Prince's body. Jesus' chest rose as He drew in His first new breath.

Ariel and Tobias exchanged a thunderstruck glance, then rushed toward Him, intending to tear the confining wrappings from Him. But before they could reach Him, He sat up on the slab, His body coming through the graveclothes, leaving them lying undisturbed.

Jesus smiled up at His two guardians. "Good morning."

Ariel, tears streaming down his face, fell to his knees and returned his Sovereign's greeting. "It's the best morning, Lord!"

Tobias knelt before Jesus. "It is so good to see you free again, Lord. Ariel and I will escort you Home now."

"I won't be going Home for another forty days, Tobias. There are still some things I must take care of down here."

Jesus reached for the robe Tobias was holding. Ariel fastened the sandals on His feet.

Tobias smiled at the despair he had felt only a few hours ago. "I thought these clothes might have been for a state funeral. I'm so glad I was mistaken. I wish I could have seen Lucifer's face when you were set free.

Your Father and you must have taken all the joy out of his day."

"We also took his keys. And you're right. He is the unhappiest creature on the planet this morning; and when the high priest finds out that killing me was futile, he is going to be almost as unhappy as Lucifer." He stood up and motioned for the angels to rise. "It feels wonderful to be free again."

"I know a little about how you feel, Lord," Ariel answered. "Tobias and I were detained for a while on Crucifixion Day."

"Detained? Where?"

"Heaven, Sir. Your Father put us in what He called preventive detention."

"Ariel, that is a polite term for house arrest. What did you do?"

"Nothing, Lord." At Jesus' skeptical smile, Ariel argued his case further. "Lord, I know guilty people say they didn't do anything, but innocent people say that, too. We didn't *do* anything."

"Very well. What did my Father arrest you for not doing?"

"Because we had been especially close to you-- protecting you for so many years--the King thought we might try to stop the Crucifixion."

"Ariel," Jesus said gently, "you should not have even thought about going against my Father."

"I don't suppose we really would have rebelled against Him, Lord. But when we saw how much you were suffering, and how much it hurt Him because He couldn't help you, we felt like killing every Roman and Pharisee on that hillside."

"I'm glad you didn't. However, I have no objection to your giving a certain Roman guard unit a very memorable experience. In fact, I insist upon it. Does that idea appeal to you?"

Ariel's face lit up with a huge smile. "Immensely, Your Highness. What do you want me to do?"

"After I leave here, my Father will send an earthquake. When it hits, move the stone away from the entrance, and make yourself very visible to the soldiers. I want them to understand that this earthquake is no natural occurrence. Satan had the ground knocked from under him this morning, but that quake didn't reach the surface. This one should get everyone's attention." Jesus picked up the napkin that had been tied around

His head. He folded it carefully and laid it in a place separate from the wrappings. "I intend to make sure everyone knows I left this place under my own power, and I don't think even Caiaphas will believe a tidy grave robber. Tobias, some of the women will be coming to the tomb soon. I want you to wait here for them and tell them not to look for me here. Tell them also to give my disciples a message to meet me in Galilee." Christ embraced His two protectors. "Thank you for staying the course so faithfully for the last thirty-three years. After this morning you may return Home. No one can harm me now, and you have certainly earned a rest. I will see you again forty days from now."

Jesus walked through the stone. Ariel stood waiting by the door. He felt the beginning vibrations as the earth quivered. The vibrations grew into tremors, and the tremors swelled to a thunderous roar.

Ariel assumed invisibility, then ascended through the ceiling of the tomb, pausing two hundred feet above the ground.

The Roman soldiers, more fearful of the penalty their superiors would inflict for desertion than they were of the earthquake, stood their ground as the earth shook.

Ariel shed his cloak of invisibility, and his robe took on its usual blazing whiteness. He began a slow, majestic descent. One of the soldiers caught sight of him and called out to the others. They stood rock still, mouths open and sandals bolted to the ground by fear. Ariel gave the huge stone a light push with one hand, and tons of rock rumbled away from the door.

The angel seated himself regally atop the stone and looked down at the petrified soldiers. One guard, gripped by pure terror, sank to the ground in a profound faint. His fellow soldiers joined him on the ground in a matter of seconds.

Tobias appeared beside Ariel and peered down at the now unconscious guards. "Ariel, I congratulate you. The Prince told you to give them a very memorable experience, and I think they will remember this for a long time to come. When they awaken. His Highness said the women will be here soon. Let's go back inside and wait for them. It will be nice to be able to give someone good news, for a change."

Mary stumbled through the dimness of the garden, her vision blurred by the shadows of the trees and by her tears.

She stopped short at the sight of the open tomb. The great stone that had covered the door was leaning against the outside of the tomb, several feet from the entrance.

Mary began running, fleeing down the road to Jerusalem, her heart pounding and her breath coming in gasps. She followed the narrow stone street to the house where Peter and John had taken refuge from the Romans and began pounding on the door. John cautiously peeked out the window, then opened the door for her. John's youthful face had aged considerably in the last few days.

"Who is it, John?" Peter asked from the top of the stairs.

"It's Mary."

"Mary, be quiet," Peter cautioned. "We don't want to draw the soldiers here."

"Peter, I've just come from the garden. The Lord's tomb has been opened."

The gruff, burly fisherman took the stairs two at a time and brushed past Mary as he left the house. She and John followed, straining to keep up with him.

When they neared the door of the tomb, Peter and Mary stopped to catch their breath. John ran by them.

Lingering outside the door, he stooped and looked in. Nothing but grave clothes stiff with dried blood.

Peter pushed around John and walked into the tomb. John followed him, while Mary waited outside.

John's shoulders sagged in defeat. *That snake of a Caiaphas. How am I going to tell the Lord's mother that she doesn't even have her Son's body left?*

Peter and John left for Jerusalem, but Mary refused to leave with them. She forced her feet to the door and looked inside.

Two young men in white were sitting on the stone slab where Jesus' body had lain. Mary, too beaten down by grief and loss to be afraid, stared at the two men.

"Why are you weeping?" Tobias asked.

Her words tumbled out, mingled with sobs. "Because they have taken away my Lord."

Mary turned to leave. She straightened up as she emerged from the low doorway. Another young man in a white robe stood near the entrance. Only the gardener who tended Joseph of Arimathea's private garden would be here alone this early.

"Why are you crying?" the man asked. "Whom are you seeking?"

Son of My Love

"My Lord's body is gone, and I don't know where they have taken Him. Please, Sir, if you have removed Him, tell me where He is so I may take Him away from there."

"Mary." The familiar, beloved voice speaking her name cut through her grief like sunlight cutting through fog.

"Master!" She fell on her face in blissful worship, and clung to His ankles as if He would vanish forever if she let Him go.

"Mary, don't cling to me," He said kindly. "There is so much I must attend to before I leave Earth, and I want desperately to go Home and see my Father again." He helped her to her feet. "Go and tell my disciples that I will be going back to my Father, and their Father, and I must meet with them."

Jesus' mother carried a bucket of water along the path to the house. John had taken her into his home, in accordance with Jesus' dying request. He had done everything he could to make her comfortable, and he treated her with dignity. Still, she missed the house in Nazareth where she had lived since she and Jesus and Joseph had returned from Egypt almost thirty years ago.

It had been wise of her Son to tell her to go home
with John. James and her other three remaining sons
had always considered Jesus' ministry dangerous folly,
and His murder at the hands of the Sanhedrin had
reinforced that attitude. Jesus had not wanted her to live
out her remaining years in such a tense, unhappy
situation.

His earthly possessions He had left behind at the
Nazareth house. The only thing she had left that had
belonged to Him was the blue and white prayer shawl
Abigail had woven for Him. He had worn it ever since
she had given it to Him ten years ago. The frayed shawl
had slipped from His shoulders as He had left Caiaphas'
house. John had snatched it from the street and
returned it to her after Jesus' burial.

John and the other disciples, trying to put their lives
back together, had gone back to their former
occupations. He and the other fishermen had been out
on the Sea of Galilee all night. They should be returning
to shore soon.

Mary carried the bucket through the door. It was still
early enough for the fig tree outside the window to make
the room dusky with shadows. As she struggled to lift

the heavy bucket onto a shelf, a man's arm reached from behind her to take the bucket from her.

"Good morning, mother. I'll take that for you."

"You're home early, John." Her breath caught in her throat. The arm lifting the bucket to the shelf wore a deep scar in the wrist. She whirled around. Her hand flew to her mouth. The young man reaching out to take her in His arms was not John.

"Jesus!" Mary stood frozen in place, not daring to trust what her eyes were telling her.

He smiled at her reluctance to believe. "Mother, where are your manners? I said 'Good morning.'"

She reached out a trembling hand to touch His arm, half expecting her hand to go through that arm. Her hand came to rest on a strong arm that was the result of years of steady labor. "You're real!"

"Of course I'm real. I'm as solid as you are."

Mary finally, joyfully, accepted the truth of her Son's Resurrection. She fell into His arms the way she had done in Nazareth ten years ago, when she had first learned what His future held. This time, her tears welled up from sheer joy.

"When I saw the scar in your wrist, I thought you might be a ghost."

"Mother, I told you ten years ago that I would rise from the dead," He said patiently. "Besides, you would have nothing to fear from me even if I were a ghost. I didn't want to startle you any more than necessary, and this was the best way to approach you. If you had heard my voice without seeing me, you would have been more certain I was a ghost."

Mary dried her tears with the edge of her scarf. "I don't know why I'm so surprised. You always did everything else you said you would do." She smiled at the whimsical thought that had just crossed her mind. "That robe is too beautiful to stain with tears. I've never seen linen that fine, or that white."

"A gift from my Father. It was waiting for me in the tomb."

She reached up and stroked her Son's face, checking to make certain His injuries were completely healed. "The last time I saw you, they were laying your body in the tomb. Your face was battered beyond recognition, and your back was nothing but a mass of bloody ribbons. Only God could raise you up, and heal that kind of damage without leaving a trace. But why has He left the scars in your wrists?"

"He told me I would need them to identify myself. Some of the disciples might need evidence to support their faith at first."

"It's so wonderful to have you with me again, more than I can say. Elizabeth and Joanna were crushed when you were arrested. Elizabeth couldn't bring herself to tell Ruth."

"She won't have to now. I'll tell Ruth myself what happened. Children discern things better than adults think they do."

"Sometimes I just can't understand the way your brothers think. I don't know how they're going to react."

"I do. Don't worry about my brothers, mother. I have plans for them, especially James and Judas." He held her hands in His. "Mother, I will be here another forty days, then I'll be leaving. I will be gone for a long, long time. I want you to stay with John. He will take good care of you."

"I want to go with you," Mary pleaded. "I'm so tired of saying goodbye to you."

"You can't go with me this time, mother. No one can." Jesus took her in His arms again. "I will prepare a home for you. I promise you, the next time you see me after I leave the earth, you will never be separated from me again. Not by distance, not by death, not by anything."

CHAPTER SIXTEEN

Ascension

THE EARTH FALLS AWAY BELOW; blue skies arch
overhead.

He can see the green field where hungry thousands
were fed.

Near the city, a barren hill and an empty grave.

Looking up at Him, faces of those He came to save.

Magdalene, Zaccheus, the woman from the well;

Jairus, His disciples, each with a story to tell.

Tell it they will, setting the world afire with His name.

Rome, and nations unborn, will shine with that holy
flame.

Faces blend into a crowd. His mother smiles through
tears.

She waves a last goodbye, one of many down the years.
Fading Earth is dear to Him, but Home is dearer still.
It is over, this longing not even death could kill.
Home! The very cloud that carries Him there seems to sing.
He takes with Him a gift, one that only He can bring.
For His Father, He brings the lost key to Paradise.
Lost by Adam, recovered at a terrible price.
Bought with His blood, tears, and will, this key that sets man free.
Man need not fear death, nor tremble at eternity.
It is a worthy gift to place in His Father's hand.
Love's cost was high, but He holds this key, for God and man.
Through measureless space alive with swirling galaxies,
The works of His fingers--Saturn's rings, the Pleiades.
Past Orion, whom He had designed and set in place.
God had helped Him build, a proud-Father smile on His face.
The curve of the earth is gone now; nothing green remains.

He soars northward, watching constellations in their dance,

Covering light years of distance man can't live to sail.

Vastness and blackness shield Heaven like a temple veil.

Darkness begins to grow pale, yielding way to faint light.

High, shining walls and towers now put darkness to flight.

His feet touch the pavement; the great central gate swings wide.

Michael and Gabriel bow low as He steps inside.

His gaze drinks it all in, gold columns and endless halls.

The river throws dancing, sparkling lights across the walls.

Roses bloom twice, in their reflections and on the shore.

It is all still there, unchanged from His life here before.

Phalanxes of angels, as far as the eye can see,

Stand at attention. Their song begins, sublime and free.

He looks up at the Throne Room, but His Father is gone.

Where is God? He promised He would welcome His Son Home.

Satan had whispered when He left Earth, "You don't belong.

Heaven is a foreign land. You have been gone too long."

Strong arms enfold Him. Light streams from around and above.

His Father's voice speaks. "Welcome Home, Son of my love."

He returns His Father's embrace. Safely Home at last.

His head rests on God's shoulder. Triumph swallows the past.

He places in God's hand the Calvary-purchased key.

"The world shall praise you, my Son, for you kept faith with me.

You knew my kingdom was yours, not something to be earned.

What you bore was done for love. That love will be returned

By all who will find refuge here--all who walk your way.

They will stand within these walls, reborn children of day.

The world cannot stop their march, as it could not stop you.

They see a distant splendor, and walk with Home in view.

But that bright day is distant; that time is yet to come.

For this day, this moment, my own dear Son, welcome Home."

CHAPTER SEVENTEEN

New Rome, New Jerusalem

FROM OUT OF TOMORROW come the thundering
hoofbeats of the great white horse.
Through skies reddened by the flames of new
persecutions he follows the course.
Across parched plains dry of hope, seared by doubt;
through dusty, shifting clouds of fear,
Beneath skies where vultures circle, the horse heeds
the voice only he can hear.
Forward at his Prince's call, 'mid howling, black-
souled demons he plunges on.
His hooves strike iron chains where the imprisoned
faithful hope for coming dawn.
Sparks fly upward from chains and stone prison walls,
leaving trails of golden fire.

Son of My Love

Past a burning church sanctuary, where flames now
consume the cross-crowned spire.

For long eons he had waited for this call; for ages it
never came.

Not when mad Roman Caesars lit garden parties with
Christians set aflame.

Not when Nazi Caesar wore khaki and jackboots, his
flag a twisted cross.

At last! Today, when crosses on desert sands hold
Christians Caesar calls dross.

Now the Prince has chosen to ride, and it is Caesar
whose empire is dross.

God's mills begin to grind; divine balance scales weigh
eternal gain and loss.

Sand blows on the wind, cutting, burning, blinding,
turning sky dark and sun dim.

Crosses on the sands point Heavenward, and pierced
arms, stretched wide, reach out for Him.

The horse turns eastward, moving lightning-quick,
eager to answer the command.

Past fever-ridden jungles, where mission schools and
clinics and shelters stand.

He climbs higher, faster; clouds fall away behind him,
and stars step aside.

The lights he sees before him in the distance beckon,
call him on and guide.

With one leap forward and upward, his hooves clear
city gate and jasper wall.

In the great central courtyard stand three horses, each
waiting for his own call.

An angel carrying golden livery walks to the white
horse's side.

The horse stands patiently now, quietly resting for the
coming long ride.

CHAPTER EIGHTEEN

Armageddon

PREPARATIONS FOR WAR were underway everywhere in the City. Angels moved through Heaven's streets in orderly formations, a battalion here, a company there. There was no fear, no sense of panic anywhere. The outcome of the imminent war was a foregone conclusion. The prevailing emotion in the ranks was sadness over the plight of the frail humans who would be trapped in this coming clash of titans.

Ariel lounged against a marble column while he waited for Tobias. A few yards away, Prince Jesus was conferring with His second in command, the archangel Michael. Enemy armies from nations around the world were massing at Israel's borders. Michael, as Israel's guardian prince, was intensely concerned about that nation's safety.

Ariel would not be in one of the regular units when the battle began. He and Tobias would be where they always were in a crisis--beside God's Son.

Ariel suddenly realized he was lounging and straightened up. If Prince Michael saw him leaning against the column, the commander would have a few precisely chosen words for him. Lounging, to Michael, was a most unmilitary posture. Ariel had no desire whatsoever to be summoned into the commander's awe-inspiring presence again. He and Tobias had been accorded that honor several times before. Like many other soldiers Michael had called on the carpet, they had left the room convinced that the archangel's blue eyes were actually blue ice.

Any disloyal or disobedient angels had been expelled from the City eons ago. The matters Michael dealt with now were minor, like inattention or dawdling.

Ariel knew Michael harbored suspicions that he and Tobias felt freer than the other soldiers to push the limits because they had been Jesus' personal guardian angels on Earth, and the Prince of Heaven was especially fond of them. But the two angels did not have that attitude. What they did have was a natural talent for irritating the commander. Besides, Ariel and Tobias' closeness to Jesus had not done much to keep them out of Michael's celestial doghouse. The only thing that annoyed Michael more than Ariel and Tobias was seeing humans frequently portray angels as flower-bedecked ladies or chubby infants. That nettled the archangel mightily.

The archangels were a mystery to Ariel. Archangels of the cherub class, Michael and Gabriel and Raphael held power and position second only to that possessed by God Himself and His Son.

Michael's title of prince was similar to the human military rank of General of the Army. Every whit Lucifer's equal in beauty, power, and intelligence, Michael lacked Lucifer's colossal ego. That character flaw had sent the fallen angel spiraling downward into jealousy and disobedience, and ultimately war and expulsion from Heaven.

Gabriel occupied a position equal to Michael's; but his duties were mostly those of messenger and administrator, not military matters, though he could be a formidable warrior when necessary. Colleagues and fast friends, Gabriel and Michael had stood solidly united against Satan in his long-ago rebellion.

When Satan had failed to persuade Michael to join his planned revolt, he had then tried to drive a wedge between Gabriel and Michael and draw Gabriel into his scheme. Gabriel had made a last-ditch effort to try to turn Satan around while there was still time to change course, but Satan had sneeringly brushed aside Gabriel's friendly warning. Gabriel had chosen to join with Michael and his forces, and the course of the future was set.

Ariel stood lost in thought for a long time, remembering that time before man had first come from the hand of God. When God had first created the angels, He had set Lucifer, "the shining one", in an exalted place of responsibility and high honor. It did not take Lucifer long to become intoxicated with his own beauty and capabilities. Surely, Lucifer decided, God must have even greater things in store for him. Perhaps he would even be elevated to the same level as God's Son, with all the power and prestige of that special lofty place.

Lucifer's friendship with Jesus was short lived. He quickly grew to resent Christ. It became more and more obvious to him that the supremely handsome young man with the light of divine intelligence in His dark eyes was the unrivaled focus of God's love and attention. As long as the Prince lived, Lucifer would never have the power he coveted.

Lucifer's bitter disappointment and jealousy ate away at his soul like acid, until he finally found himself standing before God as a traitor condemned to external exile.

Gambling on God's well-known reluctance to destroy life, Satan spat out his disdain for the Prince, calling Jesus God's pampered royal heir, and swearing that he would never again bow to Christ. God's quiet answer had been a promise to Satan that His "pampered royal heir" would someday give Satan more than he could handle.

Resurrection Day had been the first someday, Ariel recalled as his mind returned to the present. Today was going to be another someday. For the thousandth time Ariel wondered if Satan ever regretted the treason that had cost him everything except his physical life. Satan's ego would never allow him to admit remorse; but down deep in the hidden places of his darkened soul, where only God and Christ and Satan himself could see, did he ever miss Home and long to be back here?

Ariel snapped to respectful attention as Michael walked past. Despite the commander's exacting standards, Michael was not cold and uncaring. He would take any risk, plunge into any conflict, to protect one of his soldiers.

Ariel smiled as Michael's appearance prompted yet another memory. In that first war, Ariel and Tobias had found themselves trapped, cornered in a courtyard by dozens of Satan's demon-angels. Grossly outnumbered and going down, they had looked up to see a white-armored Michael, his great gold handled sword striking blow after blow like chain lightning, cutting his way through the slavering, clawing mob. Desperate to escape the relentless sword, the attackers had fled, happy to head for any place where Michael was not.

"Gentlemen, it is generally a good idea to stay out of corners," Michael had advised drily. "Rejoin your unit."

That experience had taught Ariel and Tobias to respect Michael's advice as well as his rank.

With the commander well out of sight, Ariel relaxed a little and resumed leaning against the column. After a few minutes, he began feeling anxious. Where was

Tobias? If he did not arrive before Michael returned, they were both going to be in trouble, Tobias for being a laggard, and Ariel for waiting instead of hurrying Tobias along. The other soldiers who were to accompany Jesus were beginning to fall into formation.

Ariel pushed himself away from the column. Better find his partner before they both wound up patrolling the no man's land between Heaven and Earth for the entire next year. That was the only unpleasant duty in Heaven, and it was Prince Michael's favorite form of discipline.

Ariel started toward a small courtyard on the other side of the Plaza wall, where he had last seen Tobias. A stirring among the soldiers near the courtyard entrance caught his attention. He could not see the reason for the excitement because the tall angels were standing between him and the courtyard door.

The soldiers moved aside to make room for someone. To Ariel's great relief, it was Tobias. He was leading a majestic white horse. The animal's flawless coat shone in the light. A golden bridle and saddle gleamed against the whiteness of the horse's coat. The horse stood patiently, without a trace of skittishness, as the admiring soldiers milled around him.

Ariel stroked the animal's head. "He's magnificent, Tobias. Who does he belong to?"

"This is Prince Jesus' horse. God created him especially for the Prince to ride today. Quite a contrast to the little donkey the Lord rode on Palm Sunday, isn't he? His name is Orion."

Michael returned and took charge of Orion. Ariel could see three more horses, one black, one red, and one ashen gray, being led into the Plaza at the far end of the square.

A shiver ran through Ariel at the sight of the horses. The famine, war, and death represented by those three horses would not scathe him, but the thought of what was about to be unleashed on the planet far below him was not pleasant to think about.

Pleasant or not, it was the only way to liberate Earth from the tyrannical, crushing grip of Satan. God's vengeful enemy would never willingly release Earth to her rightful ruler.

To Ariel's mind, the only conflict that was even a pale shadow of this coming battle was the worldwide volcano of evil that had erupted in the middle of the last century. Millions had disappeared into gas chambers and ovens before a slumbering world had awakened to the scheme hatched by Satan and carried out by a mad paperhanger.

Michael ordered the soldiers into position. Gabriel crossed the Plaza to speak to Michael, and the two archangels talked while they waited for the Prince.

Ariel, totally at a loss to understand Satan's obstinate attitude, shook his head in bewilderment. After having been soundly humiliated by Michael in a previous clash, Satan was set, again, on a collision course with the commander. It made one wonder about Satan's notable reputation for intelligence, that he would get into another conflict with someone who had, in Gabriel's succinct phrase, "whipped him all over the cosmos." And Prince Jesus Himself was going to be in front of His army in this final battle. This time Satan would be facing, head on, the Commanding General as well as His second in command.

The Father and the Prince came out of the Throne Room and walked to the top of the stairs leading down to the Plaza. Ariel watched Father and Son as they talked. The Father's glowing pride in His Son radiated from God like sunlight.

God was motioning for Ariel and Tobias to come to the top of the stairs. The two angels looked at one another. Had they annoyed Michael once too often? Maybe the commander had decided to turn them over to the Father for discipline.

The two soldiers nervously climbed the steps. They stood waiting for the Father and the Prince to finish their conversation.

"I want you to leave Satan to me for now, Son," the Father was saying. "Don't pursue him. I will see to him myself." God turned His attention to the two angels standing before Him. "I wish to commend the two of you for your devotion to my Son. Your faithful protection of Him during His earthly life, when He was in real physical danger, helped make this day possible. He no longer needs that protection, but I want you to know that you are beside Him today as a way of honoring you for your faithful service."

Tobias, nearly numb with relief, managed to stammer, "Thank you, Your Majesty."

Ariel and Tobias followed Jesus down the steps. Michael handed Orion's reins to Jesus. Jesus' handsome face was missing its usual smile. His solemn expression made it impossible for anyone except His Father to know what He was thinking.

Jesus' face, in its earthly form, had been a special target of Satan's brutality. The scars of that bitter experience no longer showed in His face. The ordinary-looking craftsman of the Nazareth carpenter shop was two thousand years gone, completely replaced by the splendidly beautiful Prince that Jesus had been before He had stepped down to Earth.

A stream of questions ran through Ariel's thoughts. *What was on the Prince's mind? Revenge for His own suffering? Retaliation for the horrors inflicted on His followers? Disappointment at not being allowed to go after Satan personally?*

Jesus swung Himself up on Orion's back. Ariel took his place beside Him, and Tobias moved to His other side. Michael, without being asked, had graciously moved a little farther from the Prince to allow Tobias a place beside Jesus.

A trumpet blast sounded through the City's streets, reaching into every corner of Heaven, echoing off walls and coming back around to Coronation Plaza.

As accustomed as he was to seeing events take place on a grand scale, Ariel was awed by the scenes unfolding on the earth. The trumpet's call shook skyscraper walls from street to spire. Sonic shock waves convulsed placid rivers, sending towering waves crashing against banks.

Destruction lined the banks of rivers all the way to the seas. Monster tidal waves pushed gigantic ocean breakers inland for miles, turning homes and shopping malls into mounds of brick-and-splinters rubble. Ruptured gas mains, set afire by sparks from downed power lines, sent fire billowing through streets. Winds born of those firestorms lashed the loose power lines through the air like cracking bullwhips, sending people scurrying for a safety that no longer existed.

The army, with Jesus at its head, poured like an endless waterfall over the ramparts of Heaven. Behind the army marched rank on rank of believers. Millions of Christians, many bearing the scars of a martyr's death, followed the soldiers. Near the front of the column was Jesus' cousin, John the Baptist. They swept downward through the Northern sky, across limitless black expanses sprinkled with stars and planets.

The demons which for thousands of years had prowled the vast darkness scattered like dead leaves before the winged, white-robed whirlwind bearing down on them.

Ariel recognized two of the retreating enemy as part of the mob that had cornered him and Tobias in that courtyard centuries ago. The faces of the two demons had been burned into his memory. *Typical*, Ariel thought scornfully. *In the face of superior numbers, the cowards were running. They would battle such a force only if they were compelled to fight.*

Surely God would not mind if Tobias and I go after those two rogues. The Father had said their position beside Jesus today was honorary. They would not be neglecting their duty by leaving the ranks. He looked over at Tobias to see if he had recognized the two demons. He had. Unfortunately for Ariel and Tobias, so had Michael. The commander's don't-even-think-about-it glance put an abrupt end to the plan the two soldiers were formulating. Michael's expression fairly shouted his warning: Don't leave the ranks without permission.

CHAPTER NINETEEN

Peace Within the Gates

IN AREAS NOT BATTERED BY RIVERS or seas, the destruction was not so sudden. People stopped and looked around for a natural event, such as an earthquake or explosion, to explain the trumpet blast. For a few moments, unaware of onrushing justice, and caught up in the business of everyday living, they kept moving through their normal routines. A bank employee filling out false reports as a prelude to embezzlement had his creative mathematic calculations suddenly interrupted by a fast-moving figure in white. A mother whirled around as a white blur snatched her toddler son from the patio.

Michael pointed to an intersection in a crumbling downtown business district and shouted to Ariel and

Tobias, "Go!" The next instant, a robber holding a knife at the throat of an elderly woman dropped knife and purse as something white tackled him. He screamed in abject terror as he dangled, hundreds of feet in the air, from Tobias' hands. Ariel lifted the woman from the pavement. Totally unafraid and not the least surprised, she smiled up at him.

"Thank you."

"My pleasure, madam."

Ariel swerved to miss the wildly swinging end of a broken power line. He winced at the sound of the lashing wire. That sound recalled the sound of the Roman scourge as it had whistled through the air on Crucifixion Day to bring its load of agony down across Jesus' back.

The robber dangling from Tobias' hands had screamed himself into silence, having run out of both breath and strength. The magnificent creature who was holding his life in his hands was looking at him with obvious disdain, and he must not do anything to antagonize the angel.

"Ariel," Tobias remarked casually, "I do believe we have one of Satan's admirers here." He cocked his head to one side and stared at the criminal as if he were a loathsome insect. "There's nothing I detest more than a predator. Why don't I just drop him?"

Tobias' remark brought a desperation-born shriek from the robber. He clutched Tobias' robe so tightly that his fingers dug into his palms through the angel's linen sleeve.

"Tobias, stop toying with him," Ariel said impatiently. "The commander won't like it if we're gone too long. Turn him over to Raphael's Seventh Legion. They're in charge of prisoners. By the time God gets through with him, he'll wish you had dropped him. I'll find a safer place for the lady and rejoin you."

Spotting a military base a few miles from the city, Ariel swooped down behind the high fence and set the woman gently on the pavement. The startled young sentry at the gate looked around, but made no move to arrest the intruders. The brief moment when most people had not realized what was happening had passed. The Pentagon had alerted military commanders around the world that the vast army sweeping forward above every continent was not an enemy force. Attacking the white army would be useless, as well as a serious mistake.

Michael looked around when Ariel returned to his place at Jesus' side. Tobias had arrived only seconds before Ariel. Ariel slid a sideways glance in Michael's direction. The commander's quick nod let Ariel know Michael was pleased with the two soldiers' performance.

Following Jesus' earlier instructions, Michael veered to the West, taking half the army with him. The two sections of the army would circle the Middle East, meeting near Israel's center. Caught in a mighty pincer movement, Satan's forces, human and demon, would be herded into the vast plain of Megiddo. Most people knew that place by its other name: Armageddon.

Ariel could see the choppy Atlantic below him. The lost world of Atlantis, hidden from men for centuries by the great waters, was easily visible to Ariel and the rest of the army.

They moved on, past Portugal, then beyond Spain and Italy. The Adriatic and Aegean Seas came on the horizon. Patmos, where John the Apostle had been exiled.

They turned southward, then eastward, toward Israel. In the distance Ariel could see the rest of the army moving toward Israel from the opposite direction.

The colossal armies struggling for control of Jerusalem were too large for the area around Jerusalem to contain. They had spilled out over the entire Armageddon plain.

Captured Israeli civilians were being shot execution style. Brutalized Jewish women and children were being dragged away as prizes of war. Looted homes were burning. Israelis still trying to resist were being cut down by assault rifles and machine guns. Military trucks loaded with belongings from plundered homes crawled through the chaos.

Michael's soldiers began dealing with Israel's enemies with the accuracy and might the human race had seen displayed only by the most technically advanced weapons. Bolts of lightning and streams of pure white fire aimed at the enemy armies found their marks like guided missiles.

The tanks that had rumbled over the borders of Israel exploded in flames, leaving the roadways cluttered with their smoldering wreckage. Their crumpled shells blocked the roads that panicked Arab and Russian armies were trying to use to escape. Enemy soldiers caught in the supernatural crossfire died standing on their feet, completely consumed.

Jesus was moving in Satan's general direction. Mindful of God's Resurrection Day warning to never touch Jesus again, Satan fled, abandoning the demons which had eagerly done his bidding. Michael looked longingly in the direction of the fleeing Devil, obviously wanting to give chase. The demons which had followed Satan out of Hell--like an endless cloud of evil locusts boiling out of the pit--were seized and chained by Raphael's Seventh Legion. They dragged their chains with them down into the fires from whence they had come.

Jesus' feet touched the crest of the Mount of Olives, on the exact spot from which He had left the earth two thousand years ago. The ground began trembling violently. A fault line hidden deep in the mount split into a great valley that ran east to west. Trapped Israelis, their retreat protected by Jesus' army, swept down the valley to safety. Jesus watched them escape between the sheltering walls of the valley, as He had once watched the Jews of old escape between the walled-up waters of the Red Sea.

The sun went dark, throwing the enemy demons into maddening confusion and setting them to fighting among themselves. The human invaders still alive died on their feet from plague instead of fire.

The battle raged on until evening. In spite of God telling them that Jesus no longer needed bodyguards, Tobias and Ariel had at first tried to keep a protective eye on their Prince. When it became apparent that Christ was doing a splendid job of taking care of Himself, they had resumed giving their wholehearted attention to the fray around them, not neglecting to watch for the pair of renegades they had spotted on the way down.

There were still a few demons loose in the valley. Tobias grabbed Ariel's shoulder and pointed to the southern end of the valley. The two demons of special interest to Ariel and Tobias were trying to slink through the shadows into an area where they could take flight into the upper atmosphere.

Ariel glanced at Tobias. "What's the commander going to say?"

"Not much," Tobias answered cheerfully as he lifted off the ground. "He's going to be in a generous mood this evening. Besides, we're not leaving the battlefield, and it's our duty to capture the Lord's enemies."

Ariel and Tobias dropped squarely into the path of the two devils. The fugitives looked around desperately for a way out. Finding themselves cornered, they turned to fight.

They lashed out, snarling and clawing. One of them unleashed bolts of blue flame toward Tobias, who was struggling hand to hand with the other demon. Ariel pushed Tobias out of danger, then tackled the demon, dragging him to the ground. They fought until Ariel finally managed to pin his enemy's arms behind his back. He held the creature down. "Someone bring chains! Hurry!"

Tobias had gained control of his assailant. One of Raphael's soldiers helped bind the demons, then sent them to their final destination.

Sunlight returned at last, spreading over the land like a benediction. The earthquake had leveled hills and mountains, leaving Jerusalem the highest point on Earth.

Michael touched down to stand beside Jesus. "Gabriel just brought word that Jerusalem has been liberated, Your Highness."

"This was an excellent effort, Michael. You had the army perfectly trained and deployed."

"Thank you, Sir." Michael hesitated before speaking again. "I thought the daytime darkness might have reminded you of that other day. I hope it wasn't painful for you."

"It did remind me of Calvary, for a moment, but the earthquake also reminded me of the Resurrection." He smiled at the archangel. "I'm glad to see you can still resist temptation, Michael. I know you would have liked nothing better than to have captured Satan."

"All in due time, Lord. I'm sure your Father has plans for Satan that I don't know about yet. From the hasty way Lucifer left the battlefield, he must have thought you were coming after him."

Jesus laughed at Michael's observation. "He didn't even want to come into contact with me accidentally, after what my Father told him on Resurrection Morning."

"I'll find your escort, Sir. I assume you want Tobias and Ariel with you at your Royal Entry."

"Yes. Send them to me."

Michael suddenly materialized in front of Ariel and Tobias. "The Prince wants you beside Him when He enters Jerusalem. But first I want a word with you in private. Several words, in fact." They walked a short distance from the other soldiers. Michael resumed his one-sided conversation. "First, those two devils you took prisoner are among the most vicious and dangerous of Satan's forces. You are to be congratulated for capturing them."

Tobias smiled broadly. "Thank you, Excellency."

"Secondly," Michael continued, "if either of you ever again injects your personal biases into your army responsibilities, the consequences will make a year's patrol seem like a pleasant stroll in the park. How clear have I made that, gentlemen?"

"Transparent, sir," Tobias gulped, swallowing his smile.

"Ariel?" Michael demanded.

"Yes, sir!" Ariel gasped. "Perfectly clear, sir!"

"The Prince is leaving in a few minutes. Join Him. Immediately."

Michael left to find Gabriel. A stunned Ariel looked at Tobias and croaked, "Generous mood?"

"Very generous. We still have our heads."

Ariel and Tobias took their places on either side of Jesus. They walked beside Him as they and the disciples had on Palm Sunday, through cheering crowds under a cloudless, perfect Jerusalem sky.

Jesus reined Orion to a halt at the Eastern Gate. He sat there as if waiting for something His escort could not see. The gate had been sealed shut with stones by the Turkish conqueror Suleiman hundreds of years ago. Suleiman had placed a cemetery in the center of the road to prevent the expected Messiah from entering the city by the Eastern Gate. Today the graves had been removed, the ground smoothed.

The stones sealing the gate suddenly tumbled forward onto the ground. Ariel and Tobias brushed the heavy stones from the road as if they were feathers.

Jesus smiled in satisfaction at the sight of the open gate. "Stones across doors have never been a barrier to my Father."

He rode through the gate in triumph, then dismounted and handed Orion's reins to Ariel. Christ called Gabriel to His side, and the two of them walked to the site of Solomon's original Temple. The existing Dome of the Rock on the Temple mount had been pulled down into tangled heaps by the earthquake.

"I want the Temple rebuilt, Gabriel. Bring the plans my Father gave Ezekiel, and the most skilled craftsmen you can find. My foster father will want to be included. Tell Joseph first. My Father will see that we have everything we need."

"And the supervisor, Your Highness?"

"I will supervise the rebuilding myself." Jesus turned and gazed out over Jerusalem. "It seems I am a Carpenter again, Gabriel. And this Temple will stand as long as God lives."

CHAPTER TWENTY

Coronation

J ESUS SAT ON A BENCH in the courtyard of His palace, holding a sparrow in His hand and peeking into its nest to watch the nestlings cheep and flutter. He looked up to see His archangel escort for the procession standing on the other side of the courtyard. With Gabriel and Michael were Ariel and Tobias.

"Come in, gentlemen, come in."

Michael bowed low before Him. "Your Father is waiting, Your Highness."

"Then we must not keep His Majesty waiting any longer." Jesus arose and gently set the sparrow back in her nest.

"Your Highness," Gabriel said, bowing, "your Father gave each of us a message He wants you to hear before you go outside to greet your people."

"Yes, Gabriel?"

"He asked me to say to you that you have never behaved in a way that embarrassed or dishonored Him. Therefore, today, for you, old things are passed away. He bids you enjoy this day."

"Is that all of His message?"

"He said that it was a private matter between Himself and you. Something you asked Him about in Gethsemane that was of great concern to you. He also said it has been taken care of, and you would know what He meant."

"Yes. I know." Jesus' smile countered the tears beginning to gather in His eyes. "I know indeed." A faraway look clouded His face. "Gethsemane--what a terrible time. But it brought my Father and me closer, if that is possible." His smile returned. "And now it's just a distant memory." He turned to Michael. "Gabriel said you both have a message for me."

"Yes, Highness. The King requests that you remain in the Throne Room after your Coronation. He has a special gift for you."

"He has already just given me the gift I wanted most of all." He smiled at His reflection in the glass door of the portico. His pure white linen robe was adorned only by a wide gold belt. His sandals were encrusted with emeralds, His favorite gems. "What say you, Tobias?" He teased. "Do I look fit for a Prince on His Coronation Day?"

"You look fine, Lord. Besides, your Father always thought you were the handsomest young man in the universe, even when you were working in the carpenter shop and had curls of wood shavings in your hair."

"And cuts on my hands from the saw. My little brothers and sisters would kiss the cuts to heal them." He pushed back the sleeves of His robe to reveal deep scars in His wrists. "But their kisses could not heal these."

Ariel opened a silver box that was sitting on a marble table and lifted out a gleaming diamond and ruby diadem Jesus had handed to His Father when He had left Heaven over two thousand years ago. "I know your Father would be pleased to see you wearing this today, Prince Jesus."

"I think you're right, Ariel. He made it for me."
Jesus set the sparkling circlet on His dark brown hair.
"Shall we go, gentlemen?"

Michael and Gabriel moved out in front of Him to
proclaim the beginning of the procession. The two
archangels walked to the columned portico. Jesus waved
Ariel and Tobias closer to Him. "You walked with me
all my life on Earth as my protectors, you stood guard
over my tomb, and I thank you for your loyalty. You
deserve to walk with me now and enjoy my glory."

Tobias and Ariel moved to within a step behind Him.
"All your life, Lord," Ariel answered, "except when your
Father told us to cease our protection during the trial
and Crucifixion. And when He asked us to leave
Gethsemane for a while so the two of you could talk
privately."

Jesus smiled. Ariel was unwaveringly, lovingly
faithful, but his curiosity sometimes created problems.
Because of the angel's immense love for Jesus, the
Father treated Ariel's inquisitiveness with exasperated
patience. Right now, Jesus knew, Ariel's curiosity level
was rising like the temperature on an August day. He
said to Ariel as they neared the doorway, "Ariel, I'm
never going to tell you or anyone else what Daddy and I

talked about that night. I don't want to relive that misery by discussing it."

"I wasn't going to ask, Lord," Ariel said, a little defensively. "I don't want to put you in the unpleasant position of having to tell me it's none of my business."

"I appreciate your thoughtfulness." Mischief twinkled in Jesus' dark eyes. "And my Father isn't going to tell you, either, if you know what I mean."

"Yes, Lord Prince," Ariel sighed, "you mean I had better not ask Him."

Jesus stepped out into the colonnade and looked out over the millions gathered in the streets of Heaven. A sea of white-robed believers flowed through streets and courtyards. Persecution, sorrow, and death behind them, they all--the most recent arrivals and those who had been here since before the days of the patriarchs-- were in a mood to celebrate. They laughed and waved the palm branches they had brought to throw before Him, as they waited for His appearance.

Jesus looked across the seemingly endless expanse of royal purple carpet that stretched from here to the Throne Room, where His Father waited. His gaze wandered casually over the multitude of faces. To a person, those faces held only anticipation and joy. His

Son of My Love

Father had, truly, taken care of the matter for Him so He could enjoy this day to its fullest. The last tiny, gray mist of a shadow from the Via Dolorosa and Calvary was gone. He closed His eyes for an instant to voice His gratitude. "Daddy, Abba," He breathed, "thank you for your never-failing courtesies to me."

A split second before Michael and Gabriel sounded the trumpets, someone in the crowd called out, "There He is!" and a roar of praise drowned out the trumpets.

Palm branches flew over the purple ropes stretched along His route on both sides of the aisle Michael and Gabriel had created in the street. Soon the lush purple carpet was itself covered with a green carpet. People bowed as He walked past them. Some of the women curtsied.

Tobias, basking in the honor of accompanying Jesus, commented, "This is like Palm Sunday, Lord."

"Yes, except that there is no Gethsemane waiting for me this time, and no Calvary. Michael, why are there ropes along my route? No one here wants to harm me."

"Your Father wanted royal purple everywhere today, Highness. Especially along this route."

"But you already have banners and the carpet. Michael," Jesus asked suspiciously, "did you put up those ropes to keep the children away from me?"

"Lord," Michael said, sensing that he was about to become the object of royal displeasure, "they have been scampering all over the City all morning like little chipmunks, trying to find you. Gabriel and I even found two of them a block from your palace this morning."

"Why didn't you help them find me? You sound like my disciples."

"This is a busy day for you, Lord. You needed time to prepare, and some time for yourself this morning."

"My day is well under way now. Take down the ropes. If the children want to come, let them come."

"Lord, with all due respect, on Earth you only had to deal with two or three hundred at most at any one time. There are millions of them here. What will your Father say if they make you late for your own Coronation?"

"My Father said I'm to enjoy today, and I would enjoy meeting the children. There is no such thing as time here, so how can I be late?" Jesus measured His words, as if He were dealing with a stubborn child. "Michael, you take one side of the aisle; Gabriel, take the other, and remove the ropes. Now."

Son of My Love

Conceding defeat, Michael and Gabriel loosened the velvet ropes from the first of the marble posts and signaled to the angels standing at attention along the aisle. The angels pulled the ropes from the silver rings and stood holding them, puzzled looks on their faces.

Children poured into the aisle from everywhere, running for Jesus' arms. He knelt to talk to them on their level, and was promptly mobbed. Seeking royal attention, they threw their arms around His neck and pulled at the sleeves of His robe. One small boy pulled the diadem from Jesus' head and placed it on his own head. It slid down over the toddler's forehead and came to rest on his nose. Jesus carefully removed it and set it back in its rightful place. "My young friend, you have some growing to do before you can wear that."

"Prince Jesus, please," Michael pleaded, "you cannot possibly hold all these children at once, no matter how much you want to."

"Your point is well taken, Michael." Jesus stood up, picking up a child in each arm, and raised His voice. "My Father is waiting for me. Meet me at the fountain at the other end of Coronation Plaza after the ceremony, and I will talk to all of you there."

He set the two children on the pavement. Gabriel shooed them back onto the sidewalk. Michael urged the children in his path on their way, and they scattered playfully in all directions.

"Michael," Jesus called out facetiously, "why don't you use Peter's fishing net to catch them?"

Michael resisted the temptation to throw a disgusted glance in his Prince's direction. The aisle was finally cleared, and Jesus resumed His walk.

Somewhere in the great throng, a Christian musician who had died in the Holocaust began singing "Jesu, Joy of Man's Desiring." On the other side of Jesus' path, other voices, trained and untrained, took up the notes of "All Hail the Power." Other songs from other voices began swirling through the air, blending into harmony instead of clashing. The notes drifted down around Him like snowflakes of music.

"For the joy that was set before Him, He endured the cross," He murmured, echoing the apostle's words. Joy. The untold millions cheering Him now were here--safe, at peace, and blissfully happy--because of Him. Because He had pushed past His deepest fears and steadfastly set His face toward the horrors stalking Him, horrors searching with the Temple soldiers through Gethsemane.

Son of My Love

For Him, redeeming mankind had meant taking all of man's punishment, including enduring the searing flames of Satan's Gehenna for a time that had loomed, in those cursed caverns, like a loathsome, hopeless eternity. His Ascension had brought Him Home to Heaven two thousand years ago, but His Father had waited to hold His Coronation until all His followers had reached Home. Now He realized anew that His Father had planned the delay so that He could see and enjoy the full impact His sacrifice had made. Joy. That emotion flitted like a bright butterfly through His soul.

The scent of incense drifting from the Throne Room blended with distant music and the singing of the crowds. The people nearest the aisle stretched their arms past His angel honor guard, trying to touch Him. Elderly saints with serenity in their eyes, and squealing teenagers; those who on Earth had been called retarded, and renowned scientists; soldiers and homemakers and world-famous business leaders. He waved to people on one side of the street, then on the other side. By the end of the procession, He had both arms above His head at once, like a triumphant marathon runner reaching the finish line.

In a special area beside the steps leading to the throne stood His earthly family, Joseph, Mary, His half brothers and sisters, and His cousin John. Dear Joseph, who had loved Him without reservation or resentment. Joseph, who had faithfully modeled for Mary's little Princeling honor and compassion and decency. Jesus stopped and held out His hand in an acknowledgment of Joseph, then of John. He clasped His mother's hand for a moment, before climbing the stairs to the throne, where His Father waited for Him.

Emerald rainbows circled His Father's sapphire throne and His own throne, in its place of honor on the right of the throne of God. On His Father's throne sat a towering Figure whose robes glowed with a radiance that came from the Father Himself. Jesus knelt before His Father and bowed His head reverently. The Father arose, and Jesus felt the diadem being removed from His head.

"I gave you this, Son, all those years ago, because the rubies signified the blood you would shed. Now I have something more rewarding for you."

The Father nodded to Gabriel, who held a cushion holding a medallion on a gold chain, an emerald ring, and a magnificent gold crown inscribed with Jesus'

name. Gabriel fastened the medallion around Jesus'
neck, bowed to the Father, and stepped back to stand
beside Michael. God placed the ring on His Son's hand
and set the crown on His head.

"Stand up, Son."

When Jesus stood to His feet, His Father drew His
fingers across His Son's eyes. "My Word says God will
wipe away all tears from their eyes. I would not neglect
to do that for my own Son." He put His arms around
Jesus and held Him close, letting the rest of the
Coronation wait. "Your route today was not a gantlet
for you to run."

"No, Abba. Thanks to your kindness, this day has
been perfect."

The Father took a purple outer robe from Michael
and placed it around His Son's shoulders. With a sweep
of His arm He motioned for Jesus to stand at the front
of the dais.

"This is my beloved Son. Be still, and hear Him."

The crowd ignored God's call for silence and
continued to roar their adoration. The sound of their
worship crested and rolled toward Jesus in a tidal wave
of love.

"That is something you will never see again," Tobias said to Ariel, "people disobeying a direct command from God, and God smiling about it."

When the noise of the crowd finally died down, Jesus stood at the front of the platform and listened to the thundering majesty of Handel's "Hallelujah Chorus" honor Him.

The Father's face shone with pride as He watched His Son receive the tribute of the crowd. The splendidly robed ruler at the front of the platform was the same sturdy Nazarene Carpenter who had worked steadily at that craft to provide for Mary and her other children after Joseph's death, until the next son gained the skill and maturity to care for the family. It had torn the heart of God to see His strong Son lying face down in the dirt of Gethsemane, blood on His forehead, gripping clumps of grass and sobbing for deliverance from the cross, deliverance He knew was not coming.

My fair young Prince, the Father thought to Himself. *Only you and I know how deep an abyss you walked through to obey me. My whole Creation is not gift enough for you.*

God walked forward to join His Son. "I have one more gift for you, Son."

"Lord," Jesus protested, "you have given me so much already."

"In a way, all those things are not gifts. You have earned them."

Jesus looked around for the third archangel. "Where is Raphael? I haven't seen him all morning."

"He is bringing your other gift."

Jesus saw a little girl recoil in terror from something she had glimpsed across the Plaza. She dodged behind an angel for protection. Jesus turned to see what had frightened the child. The adults and older children among the people had fallen silent, but not from fear. There was a sense of satisfaction running through the crowd, a feeling of 'This was worth waiting for.'

Raphael and two angels under his command conducted a chained and sullen Satan to the foot of the steps leading to the throne. The great beauty that had once distinguished the fallen angel had long since disappeared, burned away by his bitter, unending hatred of Jesus. The giant chains wrapped around Satan had been forged by God Himself.

Raphael ordered his angels to fasten the ends of the chains to the marble columns near the steps. When the chains were secured, Raphael dropped to one knee before Jesus.

"Prince Jesus, on behalf of your Father and Michael, we present you, our Commander, this gift in honor of your Coronation."

"My thanks to my Father--and to Michael and you and your brave troops, Raphael. I am pleased to accept."

A sly smile crept over Raphael's face. "I assure you, Sir, the pleasure is ours."

God spoke to Lucifer, and His voice rolled like thunder. "Kneel to my Son."

Satan stood silent, refusing to move. God repeated His order. Again Satan silently refused.

"Lucifer, I have said that every knee shall bow to my Son, and every tongue shall call Him Lord. You will not make a liar of me. I do not demand sincerity. You are incapable of that. I do demand obedience. You will do as I command, or you will forfeit your life."

Satan grudgingly dropped to one knee, in the manner of Raphael.

"No!" God snapped angrily. "All the way down!"

Satan bowed his other knee, refusing to look in Jesus' direction.

"Now the rest of it, Lucifer. Face Him. Call Him Lord, and apologize for the way you have treated Him and His people."

Satan twisted around on his knees and looked up to face Jesus. "I offer my apologies, Lord, to you and your followers."

"If you ever commit another public act of disrespect toward Him, Lucifer," God warned, "you will not rule in Hell or anywhere else. I will wipe every trace of you from the universe. I created you, and I can destroy you." He walked toward the steps. "He is yours, Son. Do with him as you wish."

Gabriel and Michael filed down the steps behind the Father. Ariel and Tobias remained at the top of the steps. "Ariel and Tobias," God ordered, "come with me. Leave my Son to consider what He wishes to do."

Ariel lodged a cautious protest. "Your Majesty, if Lucifer gets free, he could harm the Prince."

"Those chains will hold him. Even without chains, he is no match for the Prince. Come, and close the Throne Room doors. I do not want my Son to be disturbed."

Ariel, following Tobias down the steps, returned Satan's wrathful glare in kind as he crossed the room.

CHAPTER TWENTY-ONE

The Scepter of the Kingdom

THE SILENCE OF THE TOMB fell across the Throne Room. Jesus waited for Lucifer to speak. When Lucifer remained silent, his head bowed again, Jesus finally spoke.

"At a loss for words, Lucifer? Strange--when I was a prisoner in your hellish kingdom, you bragged constantly about your royal captive."

"Silence is safer, Lord. I might say something your Father would construe as disrespect for you. He is notorious for keeping His word, and extermination does not appeal to me."

"My Father has turned you over to me. You may speak freely, as long as you maintain a minimum of respect for my rank, if not for me personally." Jesus seated Himself on His throne. "Those years since Armageddon have not gone well with you. What shall I do with you, Lucifer?"

"Unfortunately, I have nothing to say about that, Lord Prince. I don't have friends in high places anymore."

"Lucifer, you don't even have any friends in Hell, now that those people down there know how you duped them." He shook His head sadly. "We were friends once, when my Father first created you. Now look at you. You have the stench of death about you, and your hatred of me has burned your soul to ashes."

"May I stand, Lord?" When Jesus answered, "Yes," Lucifer climbed to his feet. He looked up at Jesus, and his hatred for God's Son burned outward from deep inside to set his eyes afire with bitterness. "Yes, we were friends, for a short time, until I saw the difference God made between us."

"My Father was always generous with you, Lucifer. He gave you beauty and power and intellect. You were the one who chose to throw it all away."

"Yes, He gave to me, Lord, but He lavished on you. Nothing was ever enough for you, as far as He was concerned. When I first opened my eyes, you were already there, already the center of His affection. I was His creation, but you were His Son. No one could compete against you for His love. And He was not content merely to love you. He flaunted that love--royal titles, and wealth, and demanding that everyone bow and scrape to you."

The beginnings of a smile touched Jesus' face. "In one respect He gave you more than me. He gave you an abundance of chains. The only chain on me is the one around my neck. Tell me, Lucifer, was it my Father's love for me you coveted, or the power that love gave me?"

"That crown you're wearing should have been mine, Lord. At least we could have shared your throne."

"Why? You were not even a good tactician. You started a war in Heaven without knowing the numerical strength of your allies. That is not good strategy."

Lucifer moved forward as far as his chains would allow. "Your forces may have outnumbered me in Heaven, my Prince, but I dare say my kingdom on Earth now is larger than yours. You were the one who said few there be that find the narrow way."

"And I dare say, Lucifer, that you would have quite a few defections in your ranks now if those people had a chance to escape. Go out into the Plaza and see how many of my people you can convince to join you."

"No," Lucifer admitted, "I don't think they would like Hell any better than their Lord did." His sarcastic smile revealed his growing boldness. Some of his old arrogance returned. "I trust you found my hospitality adequate, Prince Jesus? I wanted my royal guest to have the warmest welcome possible."

"A bit too warm for my taste. And if I allow you to live, I shall return the compliment. You will find Hell much hotter than when you left."

"You are an extremely stubborn young man, Lord. You would not bow to me in the wilderness, and you would not bow to me even in Hell. Not even to stop the torture."

"That lavish, extravagant love my Father has for me is mutual. I had no intention of letting Him down."

Satan pulled slowly and quietly against his chains, hoping some overlooked flaw in them would cause them to snap. When they held, the finality of his imprisonment sank in. His rabid malice, further inflamed by his frustration, began pushing him toward recklessness. Hatred warred with his desire to survive. He could survive Jesus' anger, he decided. The Son was not the intimidating Father.

"He let you down, Lord. He gave you over to me. Did you see Him and me there in the crowd that day? I had His Son in my grasp, and He did nothing."

"Yes, I saw you. You were the one spitting at me all along the road. And I saw my Father there, weeping over me. No one else saw Him or recognized you, but I did."

"I had power enough that day to make God cry. The Romans gave you special treatment. Special enough that you probably brought some of those memories all the way Home with you. Did I spoil the procession for you this morning, Prince Jesus?"

"No. My Father saw to that."

Burning to express his spite, Satan edged warily closer to the brink. "I kept some special memories of that day, too, my Prince." His hatred finally got the better of him, and he jerked furiously at the chains around his wrists. "You didn't look like the Prince of Heaven then. You looked like you had been mauled by a lion. You are never going to allow me to leave Hell again, so I will tell you now--the best part of Calvary for me was watching

God being forced to turn His back on His precious coddled Son. When you were hanging there with all that sin and corruption poured over you, He couldn't even stand to look at you. It was even better to hear you call out to Him, and He couldn't answer you. I can always enjoy remembering that, and I can always take credit for it."

An arctic silence descended on the Throne Room. Expecting Jesus to lash out with the same fiery anger He had displayed in cleansing the Temple, Satan backed away to the end of his chains.

Jesus arose and took a few unhurried steps forward. "Look at me, Satan," He ordered.

Fear, as cold as the ice in Jesus' voice and eyes, began creeping over Satan. He looked up, fear freezing him motionless. The man standing at the top of the stairs was someone he did not recognize.

"My Father may be almighty God, but He has the same love for His Child as any other parent. I never saw Him as hurt as He was on that day, and I will never allow you to cause Him that kind of pain again." He drew in a long breath. "Be warned, Satan. Hear me well. I will let you live, for now, as a warning to others. If you want to gloat to yourself over what you were allowed to do to me, so be it. But if you ever again broach that subject aloud to anyone, it won't be my Father you will need to fear. I will destroy you myself before He gets the chance. Do you understand that?"

Cowering against a column, Satan held his breath, fearing to even speak enough words to answer.

"Do you hear me, Lucifer?" Jesus shouted at the top of His voice.

His angry voice carried past the closed Throne Room doors, bringing Ariel and Tobias, the three archangels, and two of Raphael's soldiers running.

Tobias stared saucer-eyed at the sight of his outraged Commander and a quavering Satan. "Lose your temper, Lord Prince?" he gasped.

"Yes, and Lucifer has found it. Well, Lucifer?" Jesus demanded.

Fearing the consequences of not answering, Lucifer surrendered. "I will do as you say, Lord."

"Bring him to the parapet," Jesus ordered Raphael.

Raphael's two angels loosened the chains from the columns and led Lucifer to the edge of Coronation Plaza.

"Hell you chose; Hell you shall have," Jesus said to Satan. To Raphael He commanded, "Remove him from my sight."

"Yes, Sir!" Raphael answered.

Raphael and his two soldiers lifted Satan and threw him over the barrier. Lucifer fell, screaming and cursing, until the earth opened up to receive him. Through the great gash in the earth, Jesus could see the fiery glow of Hell's flames. Black smoke and human screams billowed out together before the tear in the earth snapped shut like the jaws of a shark.

Raphael rubbed his hands as if to remove dirt from them. "Well done, Prince Jesus. He deserves worse than that, but since worse doesn't exist, Hell will have to do."

"Yes. He deserves worse. He has the blood of my people on his hands. He was wrong about my Father never giving him as much as me. God gave us both the same freedom to choose. You and Gabriel and Michael took the other path, and I commend you for that."

"The three of us talked among ourselves when Lucifer's jealousy of you first became apparent. We felt, and still feel, that we are God's creations, but you are His Son. He has every right to love you as lavishly as He wishes. No one has the right to interfere with that love--not the three of us, nor Lucifer, nor anyone else. We tried to tell Lucifer that, but he would not listen."

Jesus invited Raphael to join Him on a bench. "You had mixed feelings about tossing him overboard, Raphael."

"He was once a colleague, Lord, but he embarrassed Michael and Gabriel and me, in front of your Father and you and all of Heaven. He was one of us, a Guardian. But he did not want the responsibility of behaving like one. He just wanted the prestige and authority of that position. When he started that war here, he acted like a traitor and a hooligan. We wanted to go after him long before your Father allowed. Is that all, Sir?"

"Yes, that is all. Thank you."

Raphael left. Jesus walked to the edge of the Plaza and looked over the parapet. He stood there, lost in His own thoughts, for a long time.

"Son?" His Father was standing beside Him.

Jesus glanced up at His Father. "Such a terrible waste, Lord. Some of those people are no better than Satan himself, but a lot of them..." His voice trailed off.

"Are good people who made a bad decision," His Father finished for Him. "I know, and I'm glad you have such a great heart of compassion. I can't free them, though. Redemption is for those who want it, and they did not want it. I won't force it on anyone. Freeing them would be saying that your suffering doesn't matter. It would also make a liar of me, because I told you that your sacrifice was the only way to save mankind. Deceiving you like that would violate my own nature, and that I will never do. Neither of Us has anything left to give them."

Jesus felt someone pulling at His sleeve. He looked down to see the child who had been frightened by Satan looking up at Him.

"Thank you for making the bad angel go away. He scares me."

Jesus sat down and picked up the child and set her on His lap. "He won't ever come back here again, so you don't have to be afraid of him anymore. You don't have to be afraid of anything here."

"The ring your Daddy gave you this morning is real pretty. And there are green stones on your sandals, too. Why do you like green so much?"

"I spent some time in Hell. There is nothing green or growing there. When my Father brought me out of there, I was in the tomb, and it was cold and empty.

Then when I walked out of the tomb, the first thing I saw was the greenery in the garden. Next to Heaven itself, that green garden was the prettiest thing I ever saw."

"My daddy says you got those scars on your wrists protecting me and my little brother from the bad angel. We tried to find you this morning to thank you, but two angels sent us home. They said you were very busy today."

"Michael and Gabriel are soldiers. It's very important to them that everything be orderly and on schedule. If they had known I wanted to talk to you, they would have brought you to me. Shall we give them another chance?"

"I guess so, since they were nice. They didn't scare me like the bad angel did." She smiled up at Him. "Anyway, thank you for doing so much for us."

"Little one, seeing you here safe has been more than worth Calvary, and you are more than welcome."

She hugged Him and ran off to join her friends.

"Son, there is nothing wrong with removing those scars, if you would like to be rid of them."

"Perhaps some day, Abba." He studied the healed gashes. "I have almost come to think of them as my medals."

"There are people waiting for you at the other end of the Plaza. Didn't you tell them you would meet them there?"

"Yes, and I should go join them. A Prince, of all people, must keep His word."

Jesus walked toward the waiting crowd. The Father watched proudly as people thronged His path, wanting to talk to Him and touch Him.

"It seems that our Lion of Judah has learned to roar," Tobias said to the Father. "Not only did Lucifer hear Him, but all of Heaven must have heard Him, even with the Throne Room doors closed. Whatever happened to 'gentle Jesus, meek and mild?'"

The Father looked across the Plaza to where Jesus, a child in each arm, had just finished explaining a passage of Scripture text to an elderly man. The man, pleased to have the puzzling question answered at last, was thanking Jesus for taking time to talk to him.

God smiled. The old man would remain old only a few moments longer. All Jesus' people were going to be transformed so that no one would be aged, or a child.

Everyone would be at a perfect age, at the peak of health and knowledge.

"Over there, Tobias," the Father answered. "Gentle Jesus is over there, with His people, where He rightfully belongs."

EPILOGUE

Adam waited patiently outside the gate. As he stood holding his wife's hand, memories began drifting through his mind like the soft breezes that used to play through Eden.

A perfect world, the first Eden. The animals had been friends then, and the garden awash in flowers. Perfume from the flowers would float on the breezes into every corner of the garden.

God would always join them on their evening walks, sometimes pointing out something their eyes had missed—a mother bird with a nest full of chirping babies, or a particularly beautiful butterfly. Always the proud Father, God might tell them of a new constellation His Son had set in place. Sometimes God would just listen to them talk, enjoying the delight the couple took in His Creation.

Then came Eve's foolish decision to listen to God's lying, treacherous enemy. And Adam's own failure to speak out against Satan's intrusion into their home. What whisper out of Hell had persuaded them that Satan cared more for their welfare than God did? Conceited himself, Satan had understood how to bend their wills and personalities toward pride.

The road to Redemption had led from garden to garden. From Eden to Gethsemane. Now that road had come full circle, back to this lovely place. God's grace had even gone so far that He had honored Adam by applying Adam's name to His own beloved Son. Jesus, the second Adam.

A rustle of wings brought Adam out of his reverie. An angel's feet touched the ground just inside the gate. The same angel who had held a flaming sword when they had been driven out of Eden was now holding a key. Key in hand, the angel stood at attention, waiting for someone.

Adam heard footsteps walking down the path, coming toward them. A tall Figure in a spotless white linen robe came around a bend in the path. The smile radiating from the Prince's beautiful face drove away every remaining trace of nervousness lingering in their hearts. The warmth in Jesus' eyes told them He was as happy to see them here again as they were happy to see Him.

The angel bowed and handed the key to Jesus. Christ unlocked Eden's gate and swung it open. He held out His arms wide and welcoming.

"My Father asked me to tell you welcome home. On behalf of Him and myself, come. He is waiting for us."